Escape to the Everglades

Escape to the Everglades

Edwina Raffa and Annelle Rigsby

Pineapple Press, Inc.
Sarasota, Florida

While some of the characters and the events described in this book may be based on real people and actual historical events, Will Cypress is a fictional character and his story is a work of fiction created by the authors. In particular the Green Corn Dance is a secret and sacred ceremony of the Seminoles, and this account of it is purely fictional.

Inquiries should be addressed to:

Pineapple Press, Inc.
P.O. Box 3889
Sarasota, Florida 34230

www.pineapplepress.com

Library of Congress Cataloging-in-Publication Data

Raffa, Edwina.
Escape to the Everglades / Edwina Raffa and Annelle Rigsby. — 1st ed.
p. cm.
Summary: Raised as a Seminole, Will Cypress is eager to join Osceola and his followers in the late 1830s as they battle white soldiers in the second Seminole War, fighting to remain in their Florida homelands, until a chance meeting with his white father's relatives causes Will to question his loyalties.
    978-1-56164-351-6 (hardback : alk. paper)
1. Seminole Indians—Juvenile fiction. 2. Seminole War, 2nd, 1835-1842—Juvenile fiction. 3. Florida—History—Seminole Wars, 1817-1858—Juvenile fiction. [1. Seminole Indians—Fiction. 2. Indians of North America—Florida—Fiction. 3. Racially mixed people—Fiction. 4. Seminole War, 2nd, 1835-1842—Fiction. 5. Everglades (Fla.)—Fiction. 6. Florida—History—Seminole Wars, 1817-1858—Fiction.] I. Rigsby, Annelle. II. Title.

PZ7.R4435Esc 2006
[Fic]—dc22   2005030576

First Edition
10 9 8 7 6 5 4 3 2

Printed in the United States

To my grandchildren, Jacob and Julianne Lang, whose thoughtful suggestions made our story better.

—Edwina

To my parents, Warren and Cecile Reysen, for their constant love and encouragement.

—Annelle

Contents

ALABAMA

GEORGIA

To Savannah

Atlantic Ocean

Fort Marion
St. Augustine
Fort Peyton
Old Indian Camp

Gulf of Mexico

Withlacoochee

Cove of the
Withlacoochee

Osceola's
Camp

St. Johns River

Wahoo
Swamp

Trading Post

Mary's
Farm

Seminole
Reservation

Tampa
Bay

Fort
Brooke

Kissimmee River

US Unit Camp

Panther Village

Snake Clan Village

Battle of
Lake Okeechobee

Lake Okeechobee

Ceremonial Grounds
Green Corn Dance

Big Cypress
Swamp

The Everglades

FLORIDA ~ 1837

1

Alligator Hunt

June 1837

A midnight moon cast its glow on a small Seminole village hidden deep in the Florida Everglades. While the people slept, tall pine trees stood guard over their hammock, a tree-covered island rising out of the swamp. The Second Seminole War had begun two years earlier and the Seminoles rested fitfully, always listening for the approach of white soldiers. On this June night, however, only the hum of crickets could be heard.

Fourteen-year-old Running Boy Cypress quietly left his open-air chickee and walked to the main campfire. Running Boy was meeting Billie, his ten-year-old cousin. Billie was going on his first alligator hunt. He was sitting at the fire nervously breaking twigs off a branch and throwing them into the flames when Running Boy joined him.

"The first hunt is hard, Billie," said Running Boy, straddling a log next to his young cousin, "but this way you can help with the war. Remember, we can get ammunition for alligator hides at the trading post."

"*Ee-hehn.* Yes," agreed Billie, "but alligators have sharp teeth and snapping jaws."

Running Boy smiled and gave his young cousin an encouraging slap on the back. "Just watch and learn," he advised.

Although Running Boy and Billie were cousins, they looked very different. Billie had shiny black hair, dark skin, and deep brown eyes like his Seminole father and mother. Running Boy's mother was a Seminole too, but he had inherited his white father's straight brown hair, lighter skin, and bright blue eyes.

The two boys fell silent as they waited for John Cypress, the leader of the hunting party, to arrive. Running Boy stared into the fire and recalled his first alligator hunt when he was Billie's age. One summer night his father, who was a fur and hide trader, had taken him in a dugout canoe to search for alligators. That night Running Boy had killed a twelve-foot alligator with one shot. He smiled at the happy memory.

Running Boy's expression then sobered as he thought back to other times in his life. When he was younger, the U.S. government made his clan live on the reservation. As the years passed, it became harder and harder to find small game for food and his village began to starve. Then malaria swept through the Snake Clan. Running Boy's parents caught the disease and the Breath Maker took their spirits away. Finally, in desperation, the clan left the reservation and fled south into the Everglades.

Since the death of his parents, Running Boy's uncle, John Cypress, had treated him like a son. All Seminole men were taught to take care of their sister's children, and Running Boy's uncle was no different. John Cypress was also called "Bundle Carrier" because he was the village medicine man, and he spent a lot of time teaching Running Boy and Billie the ways of the Seminoles.

Running Boy's thoughts were interrupted when John Cypress stepped quietly into the circle of firelight. He wore a belted, knee-length shirt of many colors and a plaid turban with several white egret feathers tucked in the band. A rifle was slung over his shoulder.

"Come with me," said John Cypress seriously. "It is time to begin the hunt."

Quickly Running Boy stood and reached for his spear. The annual Green Corn Dance was just days away and Running Boy wanted to impress John Cypress with his hunting skills so he would receive an adult name at the festival this year. Running Boy would then be recognized as a Seminole man and be allowed to make his own decisions.

Tonight's hunt is a chance to prove to my uncle that I am ready for an adult name, thought Running Boy. *Then I can become a warrior and fight against the white man.*

Billie was also eager to impress his father. He jumped up and pulled a burning stick from the campfire to lead the way.

Using Billie's torch to light the path, the three hunters walked through the forest to the edge of *pa-hay-okee*, the grassy water. A long canoe, made from a dug-out cypress tree, rested on the bank. Billie climbed to the front of the canoe to serve as scout. Running Boy stepped in next and sat on the low boards in the middle. John Cypress followed, jumping into the canoe as he pushed off from the bank. He used a long pole to push the canoe through the tall sawgrass of the cypress swamp toward the deep alligator holes.

"Billie, get some light over there," ordered Running Boy, pointing toward the right bank.

Billie lowered his torch closer to the murky water. He anxiously scanned the grassy river as the canoe glided along. Suddenly he spotted a pair of glowing red eyes.

"There's one!" whispered Billie, clutching the flaming torch with both hands to steady it.

Billie bravely held the alligator's gaze with his light, hypnotizing the reptile as John Cypress handed Running Boy a gun. Running Boy stood up and carefully balanced himself. Then he took aim and fired, hitting the alligator between the eyes.

"Give Billie your spear, Running Boy," said John Cypress.

Running Boy took Billie's torch and handed him the spear. After several misses, Billie finally pierced the thrashing reptile. He struggled to pull the heavy, wounded animal to the side of the canoe.

Running Boy moved next to Billie and helped him get the gator into the dugout, its tail still whipping from side to side. Suddenly, the tail hit Billie's leg and knocked him into the alligator-infested water!

Running Boy quickly took a small hatchet from his belt and stilled the writhing alligator. As he lifted the torch high so John Cypress could search the water, his eyes fell upon a chilling sight. Another pair of red burning eyes was moving silently toward the boat.

Suddenly Billie's head burst through the surface of the water.

"Help me!" he cried, his arms churning like a windmill as he frantically swam toward the canoe.

Attracted by Billie's splashing, the alligator headed straight toward him. Without a second to spare, Running Boy aimed his gun over Billie's head and fired. At the impact of the bullet, the alligator's body flipped back. John Cypress quickly maneuvered the canoe beside Billie and extended the pole to him. Billie grabbed it and held on tightly as his father pulled him to safety inside the canoe.

Then Running Boy speared the second gator and

dragged it over the side, dumping it next to the first one. At the sight of the bloody reptiles, Billie scrambled to the far end of the canoe. He wrapped his arms around himself and clenched his teeth to stop their chattering.

"Don't worry, Billie Cypress," said Running Boy, laughing at his young cousin's quick retreat. "You are much safer here than in the water."

"Two is a good number for your first hunt, Billie," said John Cypress. "It is time to go home."

The medicine man planted his pole in the bed of the shallow water and turned the canoe back toward their hammock. When the hunting party reached the sleeping village, the three lifted the dead alligators out of the canoe and dragged them through the darkness to the circle of chickees. After leaving the alligators on a wooden table to skin later, the hungry hunters walked over to the eating house. John Cypress scooped up a hollowed-out gourd of *sofkee* and drank the thin corn soup quickly. The boys broke off pieces of roasted pumpkin and ate until their stomachs stopped grumbling.

As they finished their late meal, two braves about sixteen years old entered the camp carrying a deer they had shot. The hunters deposited the animal beside the alligators on the table and went over to the campfire in the cooking chickee.

"I see Tiger and Charlie are back from their deer hunt," observed John Cypress. "We will join them."

John Cypress and Billie sat down on the logs next to Tiger and Charlie at the campfire, but Running Boy chose to sit as far from Tiger as possible. Running Boy knew Tiger did not like him. Tiger refused to accept Running Boy as a true Seminole because Running Boy had a white father. Tiger taunted Running Boy at every opportunity.

Whenever Tiger passed Running Boy in the village, he hissed "Half-blood!" in a low voice only Running Boy could hear. Running Boy knew Tiger was also jealous of his running and shooting skills, but the name "Half-blood" stung nonetheless.

The four young hunters sat around the low campfire and listened as John Cypress retold the night's adventure. He praised Billie for spearing his first alligator.

"In time, Billie will be a good hunter. He learned a lot about alligators tonight," concluded John Cypress with a slight smile.

Then turning to Running Boy, John Cypress said, "You shoot as well as your father. He would have been proud of you tonight."

"Samuel Carson may have been a good shot," interrupted Tiger grudgingly, "but he was still a white man and the white man is our enemy. The white man took the good land and made us live on the reservation."

"Why did we leave the reservation?" Billie asked his father.

"The white man wanted Florida for himself so the American government ordered all Seminoles to move west of the Mississippi River," explained John Cypress. "We did not want to leave our homeland so we traveled farther south to these hammocks. Here we can hide from the white soldiers and live off the plentiful fish and game."

"The white man keeps breaking his promises to us," said Tiger angrily. "He has brought disease and war to our people."

"Many have, but a man should be judged by the way he lives his life, not by the color of his skin," said the wise medicine man. "The Breath Maker gave the land to everyone. We must all learn to live together in peace."

"We have tried to make peace many times. Instead we have been pushed further and further into the Everglades," argued Tiger. "Now it's time for Osceola to lead us!"

Excited by Tiger's strong words, Billie ventured again into the adult conversation. "Tell me about Osceola."

"He is *tus-te-nug-gee*, a war chief," said John Cypress. "He has called for Seminoles to unite against the white army that is taking away our land."

Tiger stood up and waved his fist in the air. "I will join Osceola," he said with determination. "He is a fighter and refused to sign the U.S. government treaty. He used his knife instead of a pen to put his mark on the white man's paper of lies!"

"One day I will be one of Osceola's warriors, too," said Running Boy, standing up across from Tiger. "Osceola can use my quick feet, sharp shooting, and maybe even my English tongue."

Tiger glared at Running Boy and shook his head in disgust.

"Sit down, Running Boy," said John Cypress. "That is foolish talk. People die in war, but the hatred remains. As long as you are a boy, you must stay here and protect the women and children of the clan."

Running Boy hung his head in shame at his uncle's scolding. He knew his uncle was right, but he was tired of Tiger's bragging. Sometimes it was difficult to put the lessons he learned from John Cypress into practice.

I may look like my white father on the outside, but on the inside I am a Seminole! If I get my adult name at the Green Corn Dance, then Tiger will have to accept me as a Seminole man.

Tiger's harsh voice broke into Running Boy's thoughts. "Your uncle is right. Charlie and I will take care of any soldiers who try to attack our village. Leave the fighting to us warriors."

Tiger's boasting left a bitter taste in Running Boy's mouth, but before he could say anything, Billie asked his father another question.

"Are there soldiers in our swamps?"

"Yes, my son," said John Cypress in a serious voice. "We know soldiers are moving further south looking for us because we have seen tracks of their horses around Lake Okeechobee. They will try to capture and send us away on big boats, so we must all be watchful."

A silence fell over the group around the campfire as they pondered the sobering truth of John Cypress's words. Suddenly Running Boy felt a chill run up his spine. Through the shadows of the pine trees, he could see the outline of a man with a gun!

2

Avoiding Trouble

Running Boy quickly scrambled to his feet. "Who's there?" he called out.

John Cypress grabbed his gun and aimed it at the stranger as Tiger and Charlie reached for their weapons.

"Put your gun down," demanded John Cypress boldly.

The lone man stopped walking and slowly placed his gun on the ground.

"Now step into the light," the medicine man ordered.

A barrel-chested black man in ragged clothes stumbled into the camp. "Don't shoot!" he mumbled in a raspy whisper. "It's me, Moses."

"Moses?" asked John Cypress in surprise.

John Cypress and the others recognized Moses, a former slave who had run away from his master's plantation in Georgia. Like so many other slaves, he had escaped to Florida and had been taken in by the Seminoles. Now Moses made his home with the Snake Clan.

"You have been gone for so long," said John Cypress. "We thought you were captured and sent west. Sit down and tell us what happened."

Turning to Billie, John Cypress said, "Bring our friend something to eat."

Moses sat down at the campfire and gratefully accepted the food Billie gave him. He chewed hungrily on the coontie bread and quickly gulped down the water. Running Boy, Billie, John Cypress, Charlie, and Tiger took their places around the campfire and listened as Moses began his story.

"I went to Fort Brooke near Tampa Bay to trade alligator hides," said Moses. "When I arrived, the soldiers forced me to stay at one of the camps with the Seminoles and Negroes who had agreed to be shipped west. General Jesup had twenty-four ships waiting to take us out of Florida to the new Indian Territory.

"General Jesup promised us we would be allowed to go west with the Seminoles. But white soldiers at the fort broke their word," said Moses, his eyes narrowing with contempt. "They let slave hunters into our camps and allowed them to take some of the Negroes away from their Seminole clans.

"Osceola was there. He was furious when he heard we could not leave Florida with the Seminoles," Moses continued. "So one night Osceola slipped into our camp and persuaded everyone to run away into the swamps." A smile of satisfaction softened the features on Moses' earnest face.

"The next morning the soldiers found an empty camp. There were no Seminoles and no Negroes for General Jesup to send west."

"It is just like I said," declared Tiger excitedly. "Osceola refuses to surrender to the white man's army."

"Moses, you are back home because of Osceola's bravery," said John Cypress.

"Yes," agreed Moses. "Osceola is a fine war chief, and he understands how to fight the U.S. army. He and his warriors surprise the white soldiers by attacking quickly from the woods and then disappearing back into the swamp."

"It's true. The white man does not fight like us," said Tiger. "We are better warriors."

"Our Snake Clan is strong like Osceola," exclaimed Charlie. "We will not be forced out of Florida."

As he listened to Moses' story, Running Boy's heart stirred with passion to fight with Osceola's warriors. He knew he must first get his Seminole adult name and then find the way to Osceola's camp. After he got there, he would . . .

Running Boy's thoughts about joining Osceola were cut short by his uncle's voice. "It is getting late," he said, picking up his gun. "Moses needs rest, as we all do. We leave soon for the Green Corn Dance. When we arrive, I will report Moses' news from Fort Brooke to the elders of the council."

That night, Running Boy lay on the floor of the chickee, but he couldn't sleep.

I want to join Osceola's band of warriors and drive the white soldiers from the land. Then our clan can hunt and fish all over Florida again like I did with my father.

The next morning the whole village buzzed with activity. Everyone was preparing for the Green Corn Dance in Big Cypress Swamp where the Panther, Deer, and Bird Clans would join the Snake Clan to celebrate the new year. Running Boy helped Billie skin the alligators, and together they stretched the hides on a wooden frame to dry. Billie proudly gave his mother, Minnie Cypress, the alligator meat from his first hunt. She roasted the meat and set it out in the eating chickee for the next meal. Running Boy noticed Billie ate little of it. He knew Billie was still thinking about the dangerous hunt.

For the next few days the clan worked hard to get ready for the journey. The women finished sewing outfits made of brightly colored cloth so each family member would have a new set of clothes. They also prepared food and packed it along with their cooking utensils.

Running Boy joined the men who went hunting for meat to take on the trip. He did his best to keep away from Tiger, but one day the older brave found him alone in the woods.

"Half-blood!" snarled Tiger, spitting out the ugly name.

Running Boy glared defiantly into Tiger's eyes. He wanted to hit Tiger, but he remembered a man should control his anger. The naming ceremony was so close. He did not want to spoil his chances of receiving his name by acting childishly now. So, swallowing hard, he turned away from Tiger and started back to the village.

Once out of Tiger's sight, he began running. Running always helped him think more clearly. After a few minutes, he slowed to watch a flock of pink roseate spoonbills feeding in the marshy wetlands. Overhead, a magnificent osprey soared and swooped in the bright June sky. A sleek brown otter followed by her two babies scurried across the narrow path and slipped into the grassy water. As Running Boy took in the beauty of the Everglades, he vowed to ignore Tiger and earn his adult name so he could fight for his homeland.

The day the Snake Clan left for the Big Cypress ceremonial grounds dawned hot and humid. In spite of the oppressive heat, the villagers were dressed in dazzling, brightly-colored outfits of red, blue, and yellow. Young children chattered excitedly as they walked beside their parents on their way down to the grassy water. Everyone was eager to trade news with friends from the other clans. Running Boy helped Billie load cooking utensils and food into the family canoe. He hurried to finish when he saw Tiger and

Charlie packing their dugout nearby. Running Boy did not want a confrontation to spoil the festive day. Then with Running Boy's canoe in the lead, the entire clan was soon on its way to the Green Corn Dance.

The Snake Clan poled their dugouts many miles south through the swamps of the Everglades. The spiny sawgrass parted as the cypress canoes glided through waters teeming with silver gambusia. The tiny fish darted across the water's surface in pursuit of mosquito larvae. Red-bellied turtles lazily sunning on logs plopped into the shallow water as the Seminoles passed by.

It was late afternoon when the Snake Clan reached the hammock in the Big Cypress Swamp, where they would stay for the next four days.

"There's the camp!" shouted Running Boy. He pointed to the puffs of smoke drifting over the treetops.

Running Boy jumped from the canoe and ran ahead to announce the arrival of the Snake Clan. When he reached the camp, he saw Seminole men clearing the hard-packed squareground for the ceremonial fire. Others were repairing the palmetto-thatched roof of the Big House where the men would eat. When Running Boy spied the chief elder, he ran over and waited respectfully until the old man spoke.

"*Chee-hahn-tah-moh.* Hello," said Chief Johnny Osprey. "It is good to see you, Running Boy. Tell John Cypress the elders meet at dusk."

Running Boy nodded and hurried back with the message. Then he helped his uncle and Billie set up camp. After an hour, John Cypress told the boys they could go.

"I will tell Chief Johnny Osprey and the council about Osceola now," said John Cypress. "They must hear of Moses' narrow escape and the white soldiers' deceit."

Running Boy and Billie walked over to a field where a

group of boys and girls were playing stickball around a tall pole made from a tree. The trunk had been stripped of all its branches except for a few leaves on top that served as the goal. The boys, who used racquets, were playing against the girls, who used their hands. Both teams were trying to hit the top of the pole with the tiny deerskin ball.

Running Boy scanned the group for familiar faces. He saw that every clan was represented except for the Panther Clan. He waited until a point was scored and then he joined the game.

"Here," called Jimmie from the Bird Clan, tossing Running Boy a stickball racquet. "Make a goal for us."

When the walnut-sized ball flew over Running Boy's head, he raised his racquet and cradled it. Just as Running Boy aimed for the top of the tree, Tiger shoved his arm, causing the ball to miss the goal. A girl from the Deer Clan scooped it up off the ground and scored.

"I'll mark the point," yelled Jimmie. He scratched a line in the middle of the tree trunk where the bark had been scraped clean.

All through the game Tiger continued to interfere with Running Boy's shots. It seemed to Running Boy that Tiger had singled him out and was deliberately picking on him. Every time Running Boy caught the ball, Tiger would knock his arm or trip him. Unable to score any points, Running Boy feared his reputation as a good stickball player was damaged.

Running Boy was relieved when the Everglades sky darkened to deep shades of purple and orange, ending both the day and the stickball game. He was angry at Tiger for making him play poorly, but there was little he could do while all the clans were gathered. He did not want to start a fight with Tiger. That would only bring shame on the Snake Clan.

The next morning as Running Boy sat on a log sharpening his knife, John Cypress approached him. Running Boy stood up and waited to hear his uncle's words.

"The Panther Clan should have arrived by now."

"I noticed they were missing at yesterday's stickball game," said Running Boy.

"The elders of the council are concerned," said John Cypress. "Since you are a fast runner, the council wants you to go see what has delayed them. The rest of our clan will stay here to gather wood for the ceremonial fire. I am the Bundle Carrier so I must prepare for tonight's dancing ceremony."

"I will leave right now," replied Running Boy.

"The Panthers' village is some distance from here," said John Cypress. "Follow the Kissimmee River until you see a large stand of banana trees on the east bank. That marks the location of their village."

"I know the place," said Running Boy. "Father took me there on his trading trips."

"*Hehn-tho-sha*. Very good," said John Cypress. "Remember, we are at war. Watch for signs of white soldiers."

Running Boy went immediately to the eating chickee. He put some dried strips of deer meat in a leather pouch. Then he tucked it next to his knife in the cloth belt at his waist.

Running Boy raced through the camp and quickly jumped into his canoe. He poled through the shallow waters until he reached the palmetto flatwoods. Then he carefully hid his canoe behind some live oak trees and began running.

When he reached the Kissimmee River, he ran along the bank following the river northward. From time to time, Running Boy checked the sky. The late afternoon thunderclouds were building and a warm breeze rustled through the grasses. In the distance he could see the huge clump of banana trees.

Running Boy slowed his footsteps and then stopped in his tracks. A strong burning smell came to him on the wind and thick black smoke spiraled up through the woods.

Running Boy crept through the underbrush of palmettos and leather ferns to get closer to the village. He cautiously parted the leafy branches and peered into the camp. An eerie stillness had fallen over the village. The only sound came from the crackling flames that leapt from the chickees' roofs. Sofkee from an overturned iron pot pooled on the dirt floor of the eating chickee. Cooking utensils were strewn everywhere.

When Running Boy saw three dugout canoes engulfed in flames, he was angry. White soldiers had destroyed the Panthers' village and once again forced the Seminoles to flee into the swamp.

Just then Running Boy heard horses galloping through the brush. Quickly, he dove deep into a clump of palmettos and lay there still as a snake.

3

Captured!

Running Boy's muscles ached, but he tried to remain motionless as he spied through the palm fronds. He watched two white soldiers ride into the burning village and rein their horses to a stop. His heart beat wildly as he strained to hear what the soldiers were saying.

"Round up those stray cows, while I get that Seminole girl we found," ordered one of the soldiers in English. "I left her bound up over by those banana trees. We'll take the girl and the livestock back with us to Fort Brooke."

"Yes sir, Captain," answered the other soldier. "We've burned this village and gotten us some free animals. It's been a good day's work."

Running Boy heard the soldiers' cruel laughter and he crouched lower in the palmettos to hide. He felt his face grow hot with anger as he listened to their harsh words. Running Boy wanted to rescue the Panther girl right away but the situation was too dangerous. He would have to bide his time and wait for the right moment like Osceola did.

"Let's get out of here," said the captain. "If we head north to Tampa right now, we'll catch up with our unit tonight."

Running Boy waited until the horses' hooves grew faint in the distance. Then he cautiously stood up and looked around.

The entire village was empty. Running Boy checked the ground for tracks of the horses. He picked up their trail on the riverbank and started following them, determined to find the girl the soldiers had taken captive.

It was dark when Running Boy spotted the campfire where the soldiers had stopped for the night. A small unit sat around the fire celebrating their raid on the Panther village. They were singing loudly and passing a bottle of whiskey around the circle. A short distance away Running Boy saw the stolen cows grazing near a gumbo-limbo tree. Then he spied the girl sitting on the ground. She looked to be about twelve years old. Her hands and feet were bound with rope.

As the soldiers continued their boisterous singing, Running Boy crept past them undetected, leaping from shadow to shadow until he finally reached the girl. It was his childhood friend, Little Orchid!

Kneeling down beside her, he whispered, "Little Orchid, it's me, Running Boy. I've come to help you."

Just as he reached for his knife to cut her ropes, Little Orchid whispered, "The guard is coming!"

Running Boy whipped around and saw a soldier headed in their direction. Quickly, he shinnied up the trunk of the gumbo-limbo tree and climbed high into the branches. From his hiding place, Running Boy watched as the soldier bent down to check Little Orchid's ropes.

"They seem tight enough," said the guard. "You just sit still like you're doing and there'll be no trouble."

As Running Boy leaned closer to listen, the branch beneath him cracked. The soldier's head jerked up and he stared into the tree, searching for the cause of the sound. Running Boy pulled back into the leaves and waited. The man walked all around the base of the tree looking up into its branches. Finally he shrugged his shoulders and returned to the campfire. When Running Boy was sure the guard was gone, he climbed down to the ground. He took out his knife and cut the ropes on Little Orchid's hands and feet.

"Can you walk?" he asked pulling her to her feet.

Little Orchid took a few hesitant steps and fell. "My legs are weak," she said softly. "Leave me before the guard comes back."

"No," said Running Boy. "We go together."

He put his arm around her waist and helped her hobble toward the river. When they reached it, Running Boy glanced back over his shoulder and saw the guard coming after them. Quickly Running Boy broke off two leafy branches from a bush and handed one of them to Little Orchid.

"We will swim underwater with these branches over our heads," whispered Running Boy. "When we pass the soldiers at the campfire, they will only see leaves floating downstream."

Little Orchid silently nodded and quickly followed him into the black river. Each took a deep breath and ducked beneath the surface. Running Boy grabbed Little Orchid's free hand and they began swimming underwater. Several times Running Boy and Little Orchid came up for air and then went back beneath the water. They swam several more yards and surfaced once again. This time the faint glow of the campfire shone far away upstream.

"It is safe to get out of the river, but we must keep moving," said Running Boy, helping Little Orchid out of the water. "Can you walk now?"

"Yes," replied Little Orchid, "my legs feel better."

As Running Boy led Little Orchid further and further away from the soldiers' camp, he kept checking behind them for soldiers. When he was sure they were not being followed, he began talking to Little Orchid.

"How did the soldiers capture you?"

"I stayed behind to let the animals out of their pens and they caught me," Little Orchid replied. "How did you know about the soldiers?"

"Your clan didn't come to the Green Corn Dance and I was sent to your village to look for them. Just as I arrived, I heard the soldiers coming so I hid and listened to their talk about capturing a Seminole girl. Then I followed the tracks of their horses," answered Running Boy.

"You are very brave," said Little Orchid. "*Sho-nah-beh-sha.* Thank you."

Running Boy smiled at the lovely girl who gazed up at him. He was not sure what to say, but the look of gratitude in her eyes made him feel proud. He held his head a little higher as they made their way back to the hammock in Big Cypress Swamp.

Suddenly rumbles of thunder sounded in the distance and lightning flashed zigzags across the sky. A pelting rain began to fall, but Running Boy insisted the two keep moving.

When the storm had finally passed, Little Orchid asked, "Where are we now, Running Boy?"

"We are at the place where the river meets the grassy plain," he replied. "Are you hungry?"

"*Ee-hehn.* Yes," said Little Orchid. "I'm thirsty too."

Running Boy opened his leather pouch and shared the strips of dried deer meat. Then he picked an air plant from a branch above their heads. He gave it to Little Orchid and she drank the rainwater that had collected in the plant's base.

While they rested, Running Boy tried to reassure Little Orchid. "You will be safe from the soldiers at the hammock," said Running Boy. "Your parents know how to survive in the swamps. They will come to the Green Corn Dance when they are sure they are not being followed."

"You're right," said Little Orchid. "I'll try not to worry."

After a few minutes Running Boy said, "I know you're tired, but we must go now, Little Orchid."

"*Ee-hehn.* Yes, Running Boy," agreed Little Orchid. "I'm ready."

She stood up and brushed off the dirt clinging to her damp skirt. The two then started across the palmetto flatwoods. The moon was up when they got to the edge of the Everglades, and Running Boy easily found the live oaks where he had hidden his canoe. He dragged the dugout into the river of grass and steadied it while Little Orchid stepped into the front. Then he pushed the canoe out into the water and jumped in the back.

Steamy heat pressed down on Running Boy and Little Orchid as the canoe slipped quietly through the heavy growth of vines from strangler fig trees. Trails of Spanish moss hung down from branches overhead and tickled Running Boy's face each time the dugout passed beneath the cypress trees. Mosquitoes buzzed around their ears and bit their arms and legs. Exhausted, Little Orchid leaned against the side of the canoe and closed her eyes. Soon she was fast asleep.

Running Boy was tired too, but his mind kept picturing the devastation of Little Orchid's village.

Osceola is right to fight the white man. The soldiers must be punished for what they have done to my friends.

He poled faster and faster, energized by an anger that increased with each swing of the pole.

When the first rays of the sun lit the Everglades sky, Running Boy saw the thatched roofs on the hammock in Big Cypress Swamp. Little Orchid sat up, rubbed the sleep from her eyes, and leaned out over the bow of the canoe, straining to catch sight of the village.

"We are almost there, Little Orchid," said Running Boy. "We'll get something to eat and ask if there has been news of your clan."

Running Boy skillfully maneuvered the canoe onto the bank of the hammock. The two weary travelers walked to the eating chickee where Billie's mother was setting out food for the Feast Day of the Green Corn Dance. Little Orchid sat on the raised floor of the chickee while Running Boy spoke quietly with his aunt.

"I've just returned with Little Orchid from the Panther Clan," said Running Boy. "Her village was burned by the army and she was captured. She's been through a lot."

"Go tell this news to your uncle," Minnie Cypress said. "I'll stay with Little Orchid. She will be safe here."

Then Minnie Cypress turned to Little Orchid and said kindly, "While you eat, I will find clean clothes for you to wear. Then I will wash your skirt."

Leaving Little Orchid with his aunt, Running Boy ran to the Big House where the men were eating their morning meal. His eyes searched the group for John Cypress. When the medicine man saw his nephew waiting outside, he got up and went to meet him.

"The soldiers burned the Panthers' village and stole their cows," reported Running Boy. "They took Little Orchid captive. I helped her escape and brought her back with me. I made sure we were not followed."

"You have done well," said John Cypress. "The Panther Clan will come when it is safe. We will make plans to build them a new village."

John Cypress put his hand on Running Boy's shoulder. "Go now and rest. You want to be ready for tonight's celebration. *Tee-hee-choh-lah-gah.* See you later."

That evening when Running Boy went to the campfire, he saw Little Orchid with the other girls. She was dressed in a calico top and long skirt with a ruffle at the bottom. Many strings of blue glass beads covered her neck. She looked pleased to be among her friends again after her frightening experience with the soldiers.

Billie came over to Running Boy with a basket of white egret feathers he had found.

"Those are fine feathers for the naming ceremony," commented Running Boy.

"I wanted to find them for Father to put in his medicine bundle," said Billie.

"Sit down with me," said Running Boy. "I'll tell you how I rescued Little Orchid."

Billie put his basket down and sat near Running Boy. His eyes widened with excitement as Running Boy told him about the destruction of the Panther village and how he had found Little Orchid.

"I wish I'd been with you, Running Boy," Billie said boldly. "Together we could have saved the village."

Running Boy was amused by his young cousin's enthusiasm. "Billie," said Running Boy, "you must learn to fight like Osceola. He waits patiently until the time is right and then sneaks up on his enemy."

"*Ee-hehn.* Yes, Running Boy," agreed Billie. "There is a time for everything . . . and now it's time to eat!"

Running Boy laughed as he and Billie joined the other villagers for the Green Corn Feast in the crowded eating chickee. Billie gnawed on a turkey leg while Running Boy ate roasted duck with potatoes and squash. Then he and

Billie took large portions of their favorite honey-sweetened coontie dessert.

When Running Boy and Billie could not eat another bite, they joined their friends at the dance grounds. They listened to the men sing chants while the women danced with shakers made of box turtle shells strapped on their legs. The beans inside the turtle shells made a musical rattling sound that marked the rhythm for the dancers.

At midnight, the dancing and feasting ended. It was time for the men's fast to begin in preparation for the third day of the festival.

That night, Running Boy tossed and turned on the hard wooden floor of the chickee. He was worried about the upcoming naming ceremony.

Will I get my adult name? If I don't, Tiger will bully me even more.

4

The Silver Gorget

When the sun rose on the third day of the Green Corn Dance, Running Boy dressed in the new clothes Minnie Cypress had made for him. His fingers slipped as he nervously tightened his cloth belt. He had waited so long for the day of the naming ceremony and finally it had arrived.

As he passed the cooking chickee, Running Boy saw Little Orchid waving shyly to him. He smiled and waved back at her. Then he continued on until he found his cousin and his uncle at the medicine fire. John Cypress would teach Running Boy and Billie the traditions of spiritual healing of the Green Corn Dance that day.

"Come," said John Cypress. "I need to examine the medicine bundle before I hang it on the stake for everyone to see."

He took the deerskin bundle and opened it. "The Breath Maker gave us this sacred bundle," the medicine man said. "It links us to our ancestors and contains everything we need for our well-being. During war it is a source of power and protection for our warriors. Under my supervision, you and Billie will now prepare *Asi*, the Black Drink."

Running Boy and Billie mixed the Black Drink in a three-legged iron pot. John Cypress added button snakeroot and several other plants to the mystic brew. Then the medicine man placed the pot on logs laid for a campfire. As Running Boy handed holly leaves to his uncle to shred into the black tea, he heard shouts coming from the bank of the hammock.

"Uncle, is that the Panther Clan?" asked Running Boy.

John Cypress looked up and stared in the direction of the commotion. "Go see what is happening," he directed.

As Running Boy ran toward the canoes, he saw a weary group straggle onto the hammock. It was the Panther Clan, and they walked slowly carrying only a few belongings. Chief Johnny Osprey welcomed the elder and then showed him the chickees that had been prepared for his clan.

Many of the Seminoles came out from their chickees to greet the late arrivals. Little Orchid joined the crowd and anxiously looked for her parents. Her face lit up when she spotted a smiling man and woman coming toward her. She raced to them with open arms. After giving her mother and father a hug, she turned and motioned for Running Boy to join them.

"Running Boy rescued me from the soldiers," said Little Orchid, as he came up to them.

"*Sho-nah-beh-sha.* Thank you," said Little Orchid's mother.

"You have shown much courage," said Little Orchid's father, unfastening a necklace he was wearing.

The man paused to study the two crescent-shaped medallions he held in his hand. Then he tied the silver gorget around Running Boy's neck.

"Wear this," said the man. "It will be a sign to others that you have acted bravely to help a friend."

"*Sho-nah-beh-sha,*" replied Running Boy respectfully. "Thank you."

At that moment, Running Boy spotted Tiger standing to one side, a look of jealousy stamped on his face. Tiger's expression told Running Boy he would try to cause even more trouble for him.

When all the Panther canoes had emptied, Chief Johnny Osprey raised his arms in the air to get his people's attention.

"Now that the Panther Clan is reunited with us, the council will hold the annual meeting," announced the chief. "We have many matters to discuss that affect the whole tribe."

Running Boy spent the rest of the day waiting for the elders to finish their meeting. He tried to play stickball, but he found it hard to concentrate on the game. Running Boy even managed to ignore Tiger's bullying because he was determined to act like an adult, not a boy.

At twilight, the medicine fire was lit to heat the pot of Black Drink. It was almost midnight when John Cypress added the ceremonial ears of green corn to the boiling black liquid to begin the men's purifying ceremony.

Running Boy watched each man drink the Black Drink. When it was his turn, he took a mouthful and swallowed. As the foul-tasting liquid took effect, the men left the dance grounds one by one to vomit in the bushes, a means of purging their bodies of evil thoughts and acts. The Black Drink cleansed their spirits and gave the warriors extra strength for battle.

Billie lined up with the other little boys for their cleansing ceremony. The youngsters were scratched on their legs with a wild turkey quill until they bled. Billie stood bravely and endured his scratches because it ensured his good health for the coming year.

At midnight the Naming Ceremony began. Running Boy sat with the other boys his age in a semicircle behind the fire. He nervously waited to hear his name called.

Finally John Cypress said, "Running Boy, come forward."

Running Boy got up and walked quickly to his uncle. His heart pounded in anticipation of what his new name would be. In a moment, he would become a man!

"Will Cypress!" said Bundle Carrier. He called in a loud voice to bring forth the spirit of the ancestor whose name would be given to Running Boy. Running Boy stood proudly as he listened to his new name being called out three more times.

I have been given the name of my mother's father, a strong Seminole warrior. From this moment on, I will be known as Will Cypress! I must bring honor to this name.

Next the medicine man tied a red bandana around Will's head. Stepping over to the medicine bundle, John Cypress reached in and took out a white feather. He inserted the egret plume into Will's headband. Then Will took his place with the men and women who were beginning the Green Corn Dance. Will chanted with the men throughout the night, celebrating his new name.

At dawn the women went back to the cooking chickee to prepare food for the men who had been fasting. John Cypress walked to the ceremonial square and opened the medicine bundle to follow the yearly ritual of examining the bits of horn, stones, feathers, and herbs. When he finished, he rewrapped the bundle and put it away. Then he walked toward the Big House to join Will and the other men who were feasting on green corn, the Seminole symbol of life.

At midday all the clans gathered for their farewell prayer. The medicine man stood before them and prayed aloud.

"Oh Breath Maker, bless our people and our land. Keep us safe from the soldiers so we may return here next year."

Chief Johnny Osprey then stood and added, "We must never forget our traditions for we have shared the sacred fire and are one people."

In the afternoon, the clans said their goodbyes and began leaving the hammock. Will joined the rest of the men who had been assigned to rebuild the Panther camp during the summer months. It would be built downstream from the Snake Clan's village. As Will stood with the other men packing their canoes, Tiger swaggered up to him.

"You may have gotten your adult name," sneered Tiger, "but you are still a child, Running Boy. You must stay in the village while Charlie and I join Osceola's warriors."

Tiger reached out and ripped the silver gorget from Will's neck and flung it into the bushes. "You do not deserve to wear a medal for bravery," said Tiger, his low voice full of venom. "You will never be one of us, Half-blood!"

"Tiger, jealousy does not sit well on you," said Will angrily. "You have hated me since childhood because I can run faster and shoot better than you."

The truth of Will's words angered Tiger. The bully grabbed Will's arm, twisted it painfully behind his back, and marched him into the river of grass. Tiger put his foot on Will's back and held his head under the water. Then he yanked Will's head up by his hair. Will sputtered and spit out water, gasping for air. Just as Tiger was dunking Will's head for the third time, John Cypress came and stood on the riverbank overlooking the fight.

"*Maa-sha-ke!* Behave yourselves!" ordered John Cypress.

Reluctantly Tiger dropped Will and stomped out of the water, defiantly brushing past John Cypress. Will stumbled from the river and reached into the bushes to retrieve his necklace. He hurried to pass through the group of Seminoles who stood on the bank watching his humiliation. As he ran off into the woods, Will tied the gorget back around his neck.

Tiger shook a fist in Will's direction. "That will teach you, Half-blood!" muttered Tiger. Then he turned and jumped in the canoe with Charlie.

"You waste too much time teasing Will Cypress," observed Charlie, who poled the canoe away from the hammock. "You should focus your anger on the U.S. government."

* * *

All summer long Will worked with the Snake and Panther men. First they cleared a site for the new Panther village. Then the construction of the chickees started. Will welcomed the hard physical labor. The work made his body lean and his muscles strong. Will knew by September he would have the body of a warrior and never again would he be disgraced.

Each day as Will chopped through the heavy vegetation, Tiger's ugly words came back to him. With every swing of the ax, he thought about how Tiger had caused him to lose face with the clan. It infuriated him that Tiger and Charlie would now be with Osceola fighting the war against the white man while he had been left behind like a child.

Little Orchid was the one person who understood Will's feelings. Each day she passed his chickee on her way to get water. It happened so often that Will began to look for her. One day she stopped to talk.

"*Chee-hahn-tah-moh!* Hello, Will," said Little Orchid. "Would you like some water?"

Will nodded and took the wooden ladle she offered.

"Must you work all the time?" she asked.

"I have a lot to do," said Will, "but I have some time."

"Then sit and talk with me awhile," she said.

Will nodded again and sat down beside her. Soon Will found his tongue and began to tell Little Orchid about rebuilding her village. As the summer progressed, Will and Little Orchid became close friends. Every day they found an excuse to meet and talk. Sometimes they laughed. Other times they spoke about serious things like the war.

"It's not fair," said Will to Little Orchid one day. "I have to stay here while Tiger and Charlie fight. I want to help our people too."

"You are helping my clan right now," said Little Orchid. "Is that not enough?"

"No," said Will. "Now that I am a man, I should be a warrior."

Little Orchid frowned at his answer. Will knew she wanted him to stay nearby, but he had to prove to Tiger, once and for all, that he was a true Seminole. He gave little thought to how he would feel leaving Little Orchid.

* * *

By the beginning of September, the Panther village was finished and the day arrived for Will and the other men to return to their own clan. Will was packing the canoe when he saw Little Orchid coming to the river. He went to meet her.

"What have you decided to do?" asked Little Orchid.

"I will leave to join Osceola's warriors," said Will firmly, determination blazing from his blue eyes. "I must help protect our homeland."

Will and Little Orchid stood together for a moment drinking in the wild beauty of the Everglades. Overhead, palm fronds rustled in the warm tropical breeze as a flock of brown pelicans glided by. White and yellow orchids in the trees winked down at them like precious jewels and filled the air with their sweet fragrance. Will glanced at Little Orchid and a feeling of uneasiness came over him as he noticed tears in her dark brown eyes. As they started rolling down her face, Little Orchid hastily wiped them away.

"I will miss our talks," said Little Orchid, forcing herself to smile.

She hesitated and then asked timidly, "Will you come back someday?"

5

The Family Secret

Will knew Little Orchid wanted his promise to return, but he would not say the words she wanted to hear. He had no idea what the future held for him. How could he give his word as a Seminole man unless he could keep it?

"I will do my best" was the most Will could promise.

This time, Little Orchid's smile was genuine and it caused Will's heart to skip a beat. Before he could say anything more to her, he heard one of the men waiting on the bank call to him.

"Come, Will. It's time to go."

Quickly Will left Little Orchid's side and went down to the water's edge. He stepped into the canoe and pushed off. Each swing of the pole moved the canoe farther and farther away from his good friend. He turned around once and saw Little Orchid standing alone on the bank. Will whispered under his breath, "I too will miss our talks."

As soon as Will's feet touched the shore of the Snake Clan's village, he ran in search of John Cypress. He wanted to tell his uncle his decision to join Osceola's warriors. When Will entered the camp, he found his uncle repairing a support beam of their chickee with the roots from a strangler fig. He was lashing the ropelike plant around one of the poles to strengthen the structure. Will walked over to the chickee and picked up a long, sturdy root. Then he knelt down and worked quietly alongside his uncle. When the task was completed, the two sat down in the shade to talk.

"You no longer look like Running Boy," observed John Cypress. "This summer you have grown as tall as a slash pine."

"*Ee-hehn.* Yes, I finally have the strength of a warrior," agreed Will.

Will's blue eyes sparkled as he told his uncle his plans. He described the route he would take to the Cove of the Withlacoochee and told of his talk with one of the warriors at the Panther village who had lived for a while in Osceola's camp.

"He told me all about it," said Will. "The village is safe from attack because the white army does not dare venture into the Wahoo Swamp and the wetlands of the Withla-coochee River."

When Will finished talking, John Cypress spoke in a serious tone to his nephew.

"You are now a Seminole man. You have the right to go. But remember, your heart beats with both Seminole and white blood. Someday you may have to choose between the two worlds."

"I have chosen," said Will with conviction. "I am a Semi-nole."

The wise medicine man smiled knowingly. "Life will bring you many tests. Learn to walk your own path, respecting all men, and they will respect you."

From the advice John Cypress had given, Will knew his uncle had accepted his decision to go to war. Will had always tried hard to please the man who had cared for him and he was grateful for his uncle's understanding. Then, eager to tell Billie about his plans, Will left his uncle and went in search of his cousin.

Will awoke early the next morning with a feeling of excitement. His long-awaited journey was about to begin. When his family came down to the grassy water to see him off, John Cypress handed Will a smaller version of the medicine bundle filled with healing herbs.

"Take this bundle with you," said the medicine man. "It will protect you on your journey."

"*Sho-nah-beh-sha*. Thank you," said Will, tucking the medicine bundle in his belt. "I will carry it with me always."

Minnie Cypress gave him a pouch of food, and Billie gave Will one of his favorite feathers from a red-shouldered hawk. Will stuck the feather in his turban, much to Billie's delight. Then Will jumped into his small canoe and poled swiftly away. At the bend, he turned and waved one last time. As his dugout glided through the grassy water on that muggy September morning, Will's heart felt as light as the feather in his turban.

For the next several weeks, Will moved north on the Kissimmee River, using the sun and stars as his compass. When he reached high ground, he abandoned his canoe and crossed through a pine flatwoods until he came to the wide St. Johns River. Then he began following the river northward through the dense vegetation that grew along the bank.

Will's journey on foot was difficult. At night he slept restlessly in the woods, always on the alert for soldiers. The excitement he had felt when he left his village had worn off, and loneliness became his constant companion. He frequently talked to himself as he traveled, trying to drive the empty feeling away.

When his food ran out, he had no luck finding berries or catching fish in the river. He became weak with hunger and his imagination began to play tricks on him. At times he was sure he saw the Little People who lived in the holes of old, twisted trees. They laughed at him as they frightened away the squirrels and gophers he needed for food. It was the nature of the Little People to make trouble.

Will's mother had often warned him never to go into the Everglades alone or he might see the Little People. As a child, he had been afraid of them. Legend told there were thousands of Little People running around the ancient, gnarled trees, but thunder would chase them away. Will looked up at the sky hoping to see rain clouds. He knew he was being foolish, but it was hard to shrug off the eerie feeling that the Little People were watching him.

Almost a month had passed since Will had left the Snake Clan, and it had been many days since he had eaten. He became desperate to find food. Early one October morning when the mist was low on the ground, he left the river and went into the woods to hunt. After a few minutes, Will stumbled onto an open pasture where a horse and a small herd of cows were grazing. As the mist began to lift, he spotted a farmhouse. It had a long porch that ran the length of the building, and smoke curled from the chimney. On one side of the pine-board house was a vegetable garden filled with ripening yellow corn, plump red tomatoes, and green pole beans. On the other side of the house was a chicken coop and a small hog pen.

Will knew he should stay in the woods, but hunger pangs drove him closer. He walked through the trees around the perimeter of the farm. Behind the farmhouse, Will discovered several sheds and a barn. He decided to slip into one of the small wooden buildings and hide until nightfall. Then he would sneak to the garden and collect the vegetables. His mouth watered at the thought.

Making sure no one was around, Will sprinted from the

cover of trees to the shed's door. Pulling it open, he slipped inside and closed the door behind him. When Will's eyes adjusted to the dim interior, he could not believe his good fortune. Several hams were hanging from the low rafters. Just as he reached for his knife to cut one down, the door swung open.

"Hold it right there!" ordered a voice in English. "Now turn around slowly."

Will did as he was told. When he turned around, Will faced a white boy of about eleven pointing a rifle at him. The boy lifted the gun higher and aimed at Will's heart.

"Don't shoot!" replied Will in English.

A look of surprise crossed the boy's face at Will's response. He backed slowly out of the smokehouse keeping the gun leveled at Will.

"Come out into the sunlight," he ordered. "I want a good look at you."

"I will do as you say," said Will quietly.

He cautiously stepped out of the door into the yard. The morning sun blinded Will and it took a moment for him to see clearly.

The boy nervously fingered the trigger. Then he moved away from Will and called loudly over his shoulder in the direction of the farmhouse.

"Hey, Ma," he yelled. "Come out here. I need you."

"I'm coming, Zeke," responded a weak voice from inside the house.

A frail middle-aged white woman opened the back door and slowly came down the narrow steps. On her way across the backyard, she stopped a few times to cough and catch her breath.

"I caught this Seminole trying to steal a ham from the

smokehouse," said Zeke. "He's not like the other Indians, though. This one speaks some English."

"I mean no harm. I need food," said Will. Feeling faint, he leaned against the smokehouse to steady himself. Suddenly his knees buckled and he sank to the ground.

"Put your gun down, Zeke," said the thin woman. "This boy is weak with hunger. Run into the kitchen and fetch those leftovers from last night's supper."

At the woman's kind words, Will looked up into her eyes and said simply, "Thank you."

Zeke quickly returned with a plate of ham and cornbread and a jar of water. He set the plate and jar down on the ground beside Will and backed away. As Will devoured the food, he felt the woman's eyes boring into him. He wanted to run, but he lacked the strength.

As she continued to stare, the woman murmured under her breath. "Is it possible? Could it possibly be?"

When Will had eaten everything on his plate, he stood up and handed it back to Zeke.

Then the woman addressed him in a firm voice, "What is your name?"

"I am Will Cypress of the Snake Clan," answered Will.

"Who is your father?" the woman asked.

"He was called Samuel Carson. He died two summers ago," Will answered again.

The woman gasped with surprise.

"Ma, what is it? What's wrong?" asked Zeke.

The woman did not answer her son but continued looking directly at Will. "My name is Mary *Carson* Whitney," said the woman slowly. "I think you are my half-brother."

Now it was Will's turn to be surprised. "It can't be. I have no brothers or sisters," said Will adamantly.

The woman paused to collect her thoughts.

"Samuel Carson was my father too," Mary explained. "I didn't know of his death until you told me just now." She sat down on a stack of logs, looking even paler than before.

"How do I know you speak the truth?" asked Will.

"Maybe this will convince you," said Mary, unfastening a gold oval locket from around her neck.

She opened it and handed it to Will. He stared at the pictures inside. On the right half of the locket was a white woman Will did not recognize. On the left half was the face of his father.

"The woman was my mother. Do you recognize the man?"

"It is my father, Samuel Carson," Will whispered. "How did his spirit get in your necklace?"

"It is not his spirit. It is only a picture of him," she explained. "After my mother died, Father gave me this locket. I was still a young girl."

"Ma, I don't understand," cried Zeke. "You mean we are related to this Seminole?"

6

Seminole Uncle

"Yes, Zeke, this is your uncle," said Mary patiently. "Now please get him onto the porch so he can rest."

Reluctantly, Zeke helped Will walk around the farmhouse and settled him into a rocking chair on the front porch. Mary followed a few steps behind, stopping several times to cough into her handkerchief.

After Mary was sure Will was comfortable, she said, "I feel as weak as a kitten from all this coughing. I need to lie down for a while. Why don't you rest and we'll talk later."

Then turning to Zeke, Mary said, "Go around back and keep an eye on your two brothers. Last time I checked on them, they were heading for the barn with my milk pail."

Zeke gave Will a menacing look and stood his ground.

Mary was forced to repeat her instructions to Zeke while the boy continued to stare at Will with a look of distrust. After a minute, Zeke obeyed and slowly ambled off in the direction of the barn.

Alone at last, Will began thinking of his incredible morning. Questions spun around in his head but he had few answers. Sunrays slanted onto the porch as Will sat in the rocking chair trying to figure things out. He fought to stay awake in the warm sunshine, but his body begged for rest and soon he was asleep.

He dreamed he was triumphantly riding with Osceola and his warriors into a fort they had just captured. All the men of the white army dropped their guns at their feet as the Seminole band of warriors rode proudly past. Will could hear the sounds of the horses' hooves pounding on the hard dirt as they paraded along. The dream had barely begun when he became aware of someone jerking his arm. Will bolted up in his chair to find Mary hovering over him.

"Quick, Will, come with me into the house. Soldiers are coming down the lane."

Will jumped out of his chair so quickly he felt dizzy. Suddenly he realized the sounds in his dream were actually real horses' hooves and fast approaching ones at that! Mary wasted no time pushing him inside the farmhouse.

"Stay here until I tell you it's safe," instructed Mary as she tied on a fresh apron and straightened her blue sunbonnet. "I just hope the boys stay put in the barn. The younger ones don't know you are here, but Zeke does. I'm not sure what he'd say if the soldiers start questioning him."

Will ducked under the window and watched as three soldiers rode into the yard. Mary went down the steps to meet them. One of the soldiers started toward the porch and Will felt his heart race. Just as the soldier reached the front door, Zeke appeared at the corner of the house.

"Hey, Ma," he called. "Are they looking for Seminoles?"

The man paused for a moment and then walked back down the porch steps to talk to Zeke.

"We're looking for some renegades that burned a planta-tion north of here," said the soldier. "Have you seen any Injuns around here?"

Mary walked over to Zeke and put her arm around his shoulder. "Not recently, have we Zeke?" she said, giving Zeke the stern look she used to silence the boys' snickering in church.

"Uh, no, ma'am," the boy answered.

Then Mary turned and pointed back down the road. Will could no longer hear what they were saying, but after several more minutes of discussion, he saw the soldiers mount their horses and ride back down the lane.

When they were safely out of sight, Mary called to Will from the door and he quickly got up and came out onto the porch.

"Apparently, there was a Seminole raid on a plantation north of here," explained Mary. "That unit was looking for the group that did it."

"I didn't know," said Will. "I haven't been north of this farm."

"Of course you haven't, and all that matters is that you are safe," said Mary. "We must be watchful, however, in case those men return. They won't rest until they've tracked down the attackers."

Just then Robert and Sam came out of the barn. When the toddler saw Will, he bolted straight for his mother and hid behind her long skirt.

"Who's this Indian, Ma?" asked the other boy. Will figured him to be about nine or ten years old.

"This is Will Cypress," said Mary. "He is a member of our family. In fact, Will is your uncle."

At that bit of startling news, the boys' bright blue eyes became as round as saucers. Will understood why they wore shocked expressions on their little faces. After all, he could hardly get used to the idea himself.

Mary immediately started introductions.

"Will, you've already met Zeke Jr. and this is Robert, and my youngest son, Samuel, who is named after our father."

"He doesn't dress like us," observed Robert, eyeing Will's shirt, gorget, and leather leggings suspiciously. "He looks like us though."

"Yes, he does. He has the 'Carson eyes,'" said Mary with a chuckle. "With those blue eyes, Will, there is no doubt that you are my brother."

Mary laughed lightly and then struggled to catch her breath as another round of coughing began. Zeke jumped up and fetched her a glass of water. She drank deeply and then got up and excused herself.

After Mary went inside, Zeke called to his brothers. "Robert, grab Sam's hand. It's time for us to do our chores."

The boys walked off toward the chicken coop, once again leaving Will in his chair on the porch.

Will rocked back and forth, back and forth, trying to wrap his mind around all he had learned from Mary. In one morning he had become a brother and an uncle. He had left his village to fight against the white man, and now he found himself related to his enemies.

Will got out of the rocking chair and paced the length of the porch. He had difficulty believing these people were his relatives. His head began to swim as he sorted through all the feelings and thoughts that bombarded him. He sat back down and closed his eyes.

Hours later, Will woke up refreshed from a long nap. It took him a minute to remember where he was. He was surprised to find himself stretched out in a chair instead of the forest floor and to see the sun was already sinking in the west. Will felt something pulling on his leg and looked down to find little Sam playing with the leather strings on his leggings. Zeke and Robert were throwing a ball back and forth in the front yard and Mary was clanking pans inside the farmhouse.

Feeling Will stir in his chair, Sam stood up and raised his arms. Unsure of what to do, Will just sat there looking down on the toddler.

"You'd better pick him up, Will," advised Robert from the yard. "Sam will just keep begging for a 'horsey ride' until you do."

Will knew about that game because his father used to play it with him when he was small. He picked up Sam and gingerly perched his sturdy little nephew on his leg. Holding onto Sam's waist, Will began bouncing his leg up and down. Sam squealed with delight.

"Faster, Horsey," demanded Sam. "Faster!"

Mary came to the front window and smiled as she watched her brother playing with his nephew. After several minutes, Will looked at his sister for help, unsure of how to stop the game.

She responded with a smile and announced, "Supper is ready, boys. Time to wash up."

Grateful to put Sam down, Will followed the boys over to the rainwater cistern. He watched Zeke draw up a wooden bucket filled with clean water that was collected from past rains. After watching his nephews wash their face and hands, he did the same. It fascinated Will to see a source of water so near the house. Then Will walked back to the farmhouse with his nephews. He did not, however, follow them inside.

"Come on in," urged Mary, but Will stood his ground.

"I will eat here," he said, pointing to the porch.

"Do you always eat your meals outside?" asked Mary politely.

"Yes, that is my custom," said Will. "I am a man. Men do not eat with women and children."

Mary filled a plate with cooked beef and garden vegetables and handed it to Will, who sat on the porch floor. Then she went back inside to serve the evening meal. After supper, Will looked through the window. By the soft glow of the lantern, he could see Mary tucking Robert and Sam into their cots. When she began singing a lullaby to the younger boys, Will sat back down in the rocking chair.

Zeke opened the front door and came out with a piece of wood and a knife. He took the rocker next to Will and made a big show of pulling out his knife, making sure Will saw the blade flash in the dim light. He began whittling the stick into a whistle.

When Robert and Sam were asleep, Mary tiptoed back outside and softly closed the door behind her.

"I've been waiting to talk with you, Will," said Mary, "but we both needed our rest. If you are ready now, I'll tell you a bit more about the family."

Will leaned forward and gave Mary his full attention. Perhaps Mary could answer the questions that had plagued him all day.

"You should know, Will, that for years I have looked into the eyes of every Seminole boy who came to our trading post. I wanted to find you and it is nothing short of a miracle when you wandered onto the farm today."

After pausing to cough and clear her throat, Mary continued.

"As you know, our father traded throughout Florida. He was gone much of the time and when my mother died, he thought I would be better off living with my grandmother in Georgia. Father was not much of a correspondent, but occasionally I received a letter from him. The last letter came to my grandmother's house just before I married Zeke Whitney. It was the one telling about his new Seminole wife and baby boy. Shortly after I got that letter, my husband and I moved to this farm and Father and I lost touch. He never knew that he had three grandsons."

"Why did he never talk of you?" asked Will.

"Grandmother died soon after I was married, so Father and I had no way of contacting one another," she said. "I guess he figured that you and I would never meet so why mention it? He was starting a new life and so was I."

"Did he say anything else in that last letter to you?" asked Will.

"Father wrote he was going to raise you as a Seminole and teach you English too. Your English was my first clue that you might be my brother. Of course, it was your blue eyes that completely convinced me." Mary paused for a moment and then asked, "Since Father's death, have you been living with your mother?"

"No, the Breath Maker took her spirit away too," said Will.

"Well, who took care of you?" interrupted Zeke.

"It is our custom that Seminole uncles take care of their nieces and nephews," explained Will. "My uncle, John Cypress, did that for me when we moved to the Everglades."

"How did you come to be in this part of Florida?" asked Mary.

That question bothered Will because if it were not for the kindness of Mary, the white soldiers would have captured him. How could he tell her he was planning to join Osceola? Still, he owed her the truth.

"I am going to join the other warriors at Osceola's camp," said Will.

"Osceola's camp?" said Zeke, looking up from his whittling. "At the trading post, I heard some men say that the camp is in the Wahoo Swamp. Are you really going there?"

7

Osceola's Camp

"Oh, Will, don't go!" pleaded Mary. "Stay here with us. Your life will be in danger. I don't want anything to happen to you. After all, we just found each other."

Will heard the disappointment in her voice, but again he wanted to speak truthfully to her.

"You and I live in two different worlds," he said. "We must each walk our own path."

Mary sighed and then said slowly, "I understand why you want to fight, but if you change your mind, you are always welcome here."

Will was surprised by Mary's kind words, especially considering that the Seminoles were the enemies of the white man.

As if Mary could read his thoughts, she continued, "It makes me ashamed and angry that some white men treat Seminoles so badly. I want you to know that not all white people agree with this war. Some of my Northern friends have written that they are sending letters to the U.S. government demanding better treatment for the Indians, but Washington doesn't seem to be listening."

Mary sat back in her rocking chair to catch her breath. Will looked at his sister with concern. She was flushed and drops of perspiration dotted her upper lip.

"I have herbs in my medicine bundle," he said. "Seminoles use them for healing."

"Thank you, Will," said Mary, "but I'll be fine. Just promise to stay here a week or two."

Seeing the concern in Mary's haggard face, Will agreed to her request and Mary seemed satisfied with his answer.

"Would you feel more comfortable sleeping in that open shed behind the house?" asked Mary. "It's the closest thing I have to a chickee."

"Thank you," replied Will. Again he was struck by Mary's thoughtfulness.

Then Mary asked Zeke to fetch a blanket for Will.

"Ma, do I have to?" he asked.

"Yes, Zeke, do as I say."

When Zeke returned with the blanket, Will went around back and found the shed. He stretched out on the wooden floor and pulled the blanket over him. As he lay in the dark, he thought about all the events of the day. He was still awake when the light in Mary's farmhouse went out. Hours later he was finally able to close his eyes, and soon his head was filled with dreams.

The next morning Will awoke to the rays of the October sun warming his face and the sound of voices coming from the farmhouse. He felt much better after several meals and a good night's sleep. He got up, folded the blanket, and walked to the porch.

Soon Mary appeared at the doorway with a steaming bowl of hominy grits. Will noticed the dark circles under her eyes and how she tried to stifle her coughing.

"Good morning," said Mary, handing him the grits. "Here's some breakfast for you."

"Thank you," said Will reaching for the bowl with a dainty silver spoon stuck in the center. He used large wooden spoons in his village and he wondered how long it would take to eat using such a small utensil.

When Mary returned later to retrieve Will's empty bowl, she sat down next to him to rest for a minute. Will wanted to learn more about his sister so he asked her about the farm. Glad for some company, Mary launched into another story.

"When my husband, Zeke, and I first moved here, we stayed in a log cabin. Later when the boys came along, my husband built this home. Those were happy days. We worked hard but we had fun too. Zeke loved playing the harmonica while the boys and I sang."

"But then last year, my husband died. He was out in the woods, cutting lumber to repair the barn. The tree he was sawing fell the wrong way. It came crashing down and killed him instantly."

Mary's eyes filled with tears.

"We all miss him so. It's been hard, but the boys and I have tried to carry on. We've been growing vegetables and raising a few cows and pigs. When we need supplies, we trade a cow at the trading post."

"We were doing all right," she said, "until I came down with this cough a few months ago. It's made me weak and I just don't seem to be getting any better."

Just then Zeke stepped out to the porch and stood by his mother's chair.

"Zeke Jr. here has been a big help to me," said Mary. "Why only last week, he rode all the way to the trading post by himself to get me some cough medicine. He's the man of the house now."

She reached up and tousled her son's hair to tease him.

"Aw, Ma," he said, grinning sheepishly. "Stop that!"

Mary smiled at her son and stood up. "Well, I must get to work. Those dishes won't wash themselves."

Then she quickly sat back down and rested her head on her hand. "Mornings are usually my best time," she said, "but maybe I'll go inside and rest awhile before I clean up the kitchen."

As Mary got up and slowly walked into the house, Zeke abruptly marched down the stairs, deliberately ignoring Will. When he reached the yard, Zeke stopped suddenly and spun around.

"We're doing fine on our own," said Zeke bluntly. "We don't need any help."

"Yes," said Will. "It is like the Seminoles. Boys take care of the women and children."

Will saw a look of surprise cross Zeke's face when Will agreed with him.

"That's what Pa taught me to do," ventured Zeke again. "He gave me his gun and showed me how to shoot it, too."

Beneath the brave words, Will heard Zeke's fear. Will had felt scared and alone too when his own father had died until John Cypress helped him. Will wished he could help Zeke, but he was leaving soon to join Osceola's band of warriors.

Suddenly an idea came to him. Slowly Will untied his gorget as he walked toward Zeke.

"This was given to me for helping a friend," said Will, holding out the necklace for Zeke to see. "I want you to have it."

Zeke allowed Will to tie the silver medallions around his neck. The two polished crescents gleamed in the bright sunlight, reflecting the puzzled look on Zeke's face.

"Why are you giving this to me?" he asked.

"I am your uncle. It's a sign of my friendship," said Will.

As the days passed, Zeke continued to keep a cool distance and Will never saw him wearing the gorget again. Robert, however, was curious about his Seminole uncle and sought Will out. He wanted to know all about how Seminoles lived. Will grew fond of Robert as they worked side by side doing chores. Soon he was teaching his nephew Seminole ways of surviving in the wilderness.

Once Will caught sight of Zeke watching him from the hayloft as he showed Robert how Seminoles followed each other through the woods single file stepping in each other's footprints. The trick made soldiers think a lone Seminole was out hunting instead of a band of warriors preparing to attack. He called to Zeke to join them, but Zeke ignored the invitation.

One morning Will and Robert went out to the pasture to check on the livestock. As they were walking back to the farmhouse, Will saw clouds of dust coming from the sandy lane that led to the farm. When he pointed it out to Robert, they both ran for the farmhouse.

"The soldiers are back!" panted Robert as they burst through the door.

Zeke was kneeling in front of the black iron cookstove feeding wood to the fire inside, but he jumped to his feet to listen. Mary looked up from the table where she stood cutting her freshly baked cornbread and immediately took control. She snatched a bag from the pantry shelf and began filling it with the cooling cornbread.

"They must still be searching for the ones who burned down the plantation," said Mary as she worked. "They'll want to check every inch of this farm."

Thrusting the sack into Will's hands, she said, "Zeke will show you our secret path through the woods. It'll be faster. I'll stall the soldiers as long as I can to give you a head start.

Now go! And may God be with you."

Will saw a stubborn look creep into Zeke's blue eyes. Zeke hesitated for a minute, but then looking straight at Will, he reached into his pocket and pulled out the gorget. He quickly slipped it over his head and raced out the back door. Will followed right behind until they reached the edge of the pine flatwoods. Zeke pulled back a tangle of vines that covered the hidden path. He told Will the men at the trading post had said that the Seminole camp was less than a half day's ride west, and Will took off running.

For the first hour he frequently checked over his shoulder to see if he was being followed. When he had put some distance between himself and his enemy, he slowed down. Mary had been right. The cleared path made it easier to move quickly and Will followed the route as far as it went. Then he worked his way through the thick underbrush of the woods, heading west toward Osceola's camp.

As he walked along eating Mary's cornbread, Will thought of all the people he had left behind—his family in the Everglades, Little Orchid, and now Mary and his nephews. He wished he could tell Little Orchid or John Cypress about his new family. No doubt they would be as surprised as he was.

Will trudged through hardwood hammocks and marshy prairie lands. Will covered his tracks carefully and made little noise as he picked his way across the forest floor. He took great pains to leave no trail that would lead the soldiers from Mary's farm to Osceola's camp. By afternoon, he reached the oak tree split by lightning that the Panther warrior had described and turned north to walk along the Withlacoochee River. Will felt his original excitement return as he drew nearer to his destination.

It was twilight when Will approached the edge of the

camp and heard barking dogs announce his arrival. Will felt he was being watched and his feeling was confirmed when a Seminole guard stepped out of the shadows.

"Who are you?" demanded the guard.

Will was not surprised at the guard's curt manner towards him. His blue eyes and lighter skin always set him apart, so Will hastily spoke in Miccosukee, giving his name and explaining his reason for coming. Satisfied with his response, the guard pointed to a small chickee nearby.

"Tonight, sleep there. Tomorrow you speak with Osceola. He will decide if you stay. There is food at the eating chickee."

As the guard allowed him to pass into Osceola's camp, the first thing that struck Will was the poor condition of the village. It was not at all the camp Will had envisioned. The warriors, women, and children were all dressed in ragged clothes. From their gaunt faces, Will knew they were experiencing hard times.

Hungry after his journey, Will found the eating chickee. Unlike his clan's chickee in the Everglades, the only food available on the wooden table was some sofkee and a blackened pot of coontie mush. Using the long-handled wooden spoon, Will scooped up the thin corn drink and satisfied his thirst. He was disappointed to find the camp in such a run-down state and saw no reason to investigate further. He went to his assigned chickee to lie down, hoping the camp would look better in the daylight.

In the morning Will walked around the camp, trying to locate Osceola's chickee. As he strolled through camp, Will saw Tiger and Charlie talking to each other. Despite his problems with Tiger, Will was relieved to see people from his own clan. Immediately, he went over to speak to them.

"You look surprised to see me," said Will. "I told you I would come."

The muscles in Tiger's face tightened as he stared at Will without saying a word.

"It is good to see you, Will Cypress," said Charlie. "Osceola is weak with sickness and needs warriors. The U.S. army is becoming more determined to remove us from this land."

"I should report to the war chief," said Will. "Where do I find him?"

"I'll take you to him," offered Charlie. "Tell me about your travels as we walk."

Will told Charlie of his trip to the camp, but omitted the part about Mary and the farm. He did not want to endanger Mary and the boys by saying anything about them. Besides, if Tiger knew about his white relatives, it might hurt his chances of becoming one of Osceola's warriors.

After Will finished his story, Charlie talked to him about the camp.

"Things are bad here. Osceola has malaria, but he refuses to give in to his illness. When you see him, wait until he acknowledges you. Answer his questions briefly. If he wants you as a warrior, he will tell you."

By now Will and Charlie had reached a large chickee where a council meeting was taking place. Charlie pointed to a tall, handsome man in his early thirties standing before a group of men. His regal appearance commanded the attention of all the warriors. At his neck was a three-crescent gorget.

"Wait here," advised Charlie. "Osceola will see you after the meeting."

When the other men left, Osceola sat down and motioned Will to come into the chickee. Will's heart pounded as he stepped onto the platform to meet his hero, the great *tus-te-nug-gee*.

8

Betrayal

Up close, Will could see what Charlie had said about Osceola was true. The war chief looked sick and his eyes were glazed with the fever of malaria. Will began to shift from one foot to the other as Osceola stared at him in silence. Finally the war chief spoke.

"What is your name?"

"I am Will Cypress of the Snake Clan. I want to join the fight."

"The two Snake Clan warriors have proved themselves valuable," said Osceola, looking him squarely in the eyes, "but you are young. What skills do you bring?"

Will had already thought long and hard about this question and he was ready with his answer.

"As a child I was called Running Boy because I run fast. I can hit a target with one shot. I also understand and speak English."

"*Hehn-tho-sha*. Very good. Those are valuable skills," commented Osceola. "I too understand English but I communicate through my interpreter, Coa Hadjo. Since the white man thinks I do not understand what is being said, I learn much when they speak among themselves."

Osceola looked deep into the eyes of the young brave as if searching for his soul. Will knew his fate hung in the balance as he stood before the great war chief and waited for his decision.

Finally Osceola spoke the words Will wanted to hear. "Go to Fort Peyton," ordered the war chief. "Find out what the army is planning."

Osceola noticed Will's excitement and continued. "Leave your rifle here. The soldiers know Seminoles only wage war in the woods so they will allow you inside the fort."

After another pause he went on. "Do not speak English," he reminded Will, "or the soldiers will suspect you are a spy. I will send you with Tiger, one of your own clan. He knows the way to the fort and he is getting ready to leave now."

Will's spirits plummeted when he heard he was being sent with Tiger. He had never considered such a possibility. Will had not traveled so far to be paired with a warrior who despised him, but Osceola's word was final.

"Go now and find Tiger," commanded Osceola.

Will left the war chief and searched the camp until he found Tiger. He was leading a horse from a field where a few other scrawny animals were grazing.

"Osceola ordered me to go with you to Fort Peyton," said Will. "He said we leave today."

Tiger frowned at Will's message, but he went back to get a pony. When he returned, he threw the pony's reins at Will.

"The rules are simple," said Tiger. "I lead and you follow, Half-blood. We are members of the same clan, but I am not your friend."

Tiger jumped on his horse and galloped out of camp. Will gave his pony a kick and quickly followed Tiger north toward St. Augustine.

The two rode along the Oklawaha River and then crossed east to the St. Johns River. They kept moving and only talked to each other when it was absolutely necessary.

At night they slept in the woods. When they neared Fort Peyton, they left their horses in a stand of trees not far from its walls. As they walked toward the fort, Tiger outlined his plan to spy on the U.S. army.

"Go into the fort and listen to the soldiers," said Tiger, "while I sneak around back and count the guns. Meet at the horses this afternoon."

Will nervously entered the dusty courtyard at Fort Peyton and quickly sought refuge behind a large water barrel near the gate. When two soldiers paused for a drink, Will listened closely to their conversation.

"Those Seminoles think we're gonna let 'em stay in Florida," said a red-bearded soldier, "but Jesup's gonna round 'em up and send 'em west. He's already got King Philip and his son Wildcat at Fort Marion up in St. Augustine. But he wants Osceola too. If he can get him to surrender, the Seminoles have no chance."

"But I thought Osceola sent a peace pipe to General Hernandez requesting a meeting," said his companion. "He wants to talk, not surrender."

"Well, whatever happens," said the red-bearded man, "I just want this war to be over so I can get back home to Georgia."

As the two soldiers walked off, Will heard gunfire coming from the rear of the fort. Soldiers grabbed their weapons and started running past him. Will came from behind the water barrel and hurried out the front gate. Once outside, he began to run with the speed of a panther, swift and strong. When Will reached the woods, he found Tiger slumped over on his horse, clutching his shoulder. Will noticed blood trickling down his left arm.

"You're bleeding," panted Will. "What happened?"

Will bent over and braced his hands on his knees as he

listened, trying to catch his breath after the long run.

"A soldier caught me taking some ammunition from the supply room. He shot me as I ran out of the fort. The bullet grazed my arm, but I kept moving until I got back here."

"Let me bind that," offered Will reaching for the small medicine bundle on his belt. "John Cypress taught me how."

"I need no help, Half-blood," Tiger said stubbornly.

Will watched Tiger yank off his cloth belt. Awkwardly, he wound it around his arm to stop the bleeding.

"What did you find out?" asked Tiger as he finished tucking the end of the belt under the makeshift bandage.

"The soldiers want Osceola to surrender. Then they plan to ship us out of Florida," responded Will.

"Osceola must know of this," said Tiger, gritting his teeth in agony. He turned his horse toward the woods for their long ride back to Osceola's camp. Quickly Will mounted his horse and followed Tiger. He could see a red stain seeping through Tiger's arm bandage but Tiger showed no sign of giving in to his pain.

When Will and Tiger finally arrived at the Cove of the Withlacoochee, they were surprised to find the whole camp a beehive of activity. Most of the Seminoles were packing up their meager food and supplies. As Tiger dismounted, Will saw him grimace and clutch his shoulder.

"I will take care of the horses and then report to Osceola," said Will. Tiger nodded and stumbled off to rest.

When Will approached Osceola's chickee, the war chief weakly motioned for him to come inside and sit down.

"What did you learn, Will Cypress?" asked the war chief solemnly.

"The U.S. army wants you to surrender," said Will. "They want us to leave Florida."

"*Ee-hehn.* Yes," replied Osceola, "but I have sent a peace

pipe to General Hernandez and asked for a meeting to talk compromise. We leave today for the old Seminole camp near Fort Peyton. Tomorrow we meet the general there under a white flag of truce.

"We must meet," added the fevered Seminole with a sigh. "This war has gone on too long. . . ." Osceola's voice trailed off and Will waited patiently. Finally the war chief spoke again.

"I have information for you. Coa Hadjo brought a young white boy to me yesterday. He was asking for you. Before he left, he gave me this silver crescent with the message that Mary Whitney is dead."

Will took the necklace piece from Osceola and studied it, turning it over and over in his hand. It was a crescent from the gorget he had given Zeke.

"*Sho-nah-beh-sha.* Thank you," mumbled Will.

He tucked it into the medicine bundle at his waist. Then Osceola dismissed him with a wave. Stunned by the news of his sister's death and the return of the silver crescent, he walked slowly away.

Will wandered aimlessly through the busy camp thinking about Mary and Zeke. He had not known his sister long, but he had recognized Mary's goodness and knew they would have been good friends. All at once his mind was flooded with pictures of Zeke trying to take care of the farm and his two younger brothers alone. He wondered how long his nephew could manage by himself. Questions about Zeke's visit began to whip around inside his head like palm fronds in a hurricane.

Why did Zeke risk riding into Osceola's camp to tell me of Mary's death and give back my gorget? Does he want nothing more to do with me? If that is true, why did he return only one crescent from the necklace?

Just then he heard Charlie calling him.

"Will, get your rifle and come. We are leaving."

Will shook off his somber mood and walked over to get his weapon. Then he joined Charlie, Tiger, and the rest of Osceola's long-suffering band to start the trek toward Fort Peyton.

Jagged edges of palmettos snatched at the Seminoles' leather leggings as they followed the path east from the Cove of the Withlacoochee through a dense hammock in the Florida uplands. When they sloshed through creek beds swollen by late summer rains, thick mud swallowed their moccasins making each step difficult. An uneasy feeling came over Will when a vulture lurking in a tree suddenly took flight and circled expectantly overhead. He quickened his pace.

Finally Osceola's group arrived at the Seminole camp just south of the fort and Will helped Charlie raise a large white flag over their chickees.

"We meet under the white flag of truce," said Will. "We will be safe."

"*Ee-hehn.* Yes," agreed Charlie. "Even the white man honors the white flag."

The next day General Hernandez arrived with two hundred fifty mounted U.S. troops. As he got off his horse and walked toward the war chief, Osceola stepped forward with his interpreter, Coa Hadjo, at his side. The ailing *tus-te-nug-gee* was dressed formally for the important meeting in a blue calico shirt and red leather leggings. He wore a colorful turban with three egret feathers in the silver band and the three-crescent gorget.

Coa Hadjo presented Osceola's offer to move further south away from the white settlers and their farms. General Hernandez, however, shook his head and insisted the Seminoles surrender. Then the general raised his hand in a prearranged signal and the white soldiers closed ranks, completely surrounding the Seminoles.

Before Will knew what was happening, a U.S. soldier grabbed his rifle. He roughly shoved Will into line with the rest of the Seminoles. The cavalry formed double columns and marched the captives between them toward St. Augustine.

Will clenched his fists at his sides as he fell into step beside Tiger and Charlie. His blue eyes flashed angrily when he saw General Jesup ride up from the woods and arrogantly take his place to lead the captured Seminoles to prison.

"Hernandez and Jesup broke the truce," said Tiger bitterly as he walked slowly along, clutching his wounded arm. "Osceola acted with honor, but the U.S. army did not."

"We will never surrender to the white man," declared Will, his voice low with contempt.

"You're right," agreed Charlie. "We will find a way to fight back."

"Osceola will find a way to get us out of prison," said Tiger.

It was nearly sundown when the troops marched the captives through the dusty streets of St. Augustine. The curious townspeople came to watch Osceola, Coa Hadjo, seventy-one warriors, six women, and four Black Seminoles march into Fort Marion. Will's spirits sank when he heard the cheers from the crowd.

"Osceola is captured! Our soldiers have Osceola!"

The Seminoles were herded through the streets and over a drawbridge into Fort Marion. The high walls surrounding Will and the others were made of blocks of coquina shells and had been built by the Spanish almost a hundred and fifty years earlier. They were escorted through the courtyard into a large prison cell that once served as a store-room for ammunition. Will's courage faded a little when he heard the heavy door slam shut and lock behind them.

Will looked around his cell at the high ceiling and hard dirt floor. He felt closed in and was thankful for the small rays of moonlight spilling through the bars of a narrow rectangular window high up on the wall.

The men and women prisoners, tired and defeated, lay down on rough straw-filled sacks strewn about the floor. Will knew it was just a matter of time before the soldiers would take them to Tampa Bay and force them onto big boats. He would never see his family or Little Orchid again. He would never see Mary's boys again either. Will fought his rising panic and kept telling himself over and over they would find a way to escape.

Looking around at the other prisoners, Will noticed Tiger sitting a few feet away. His face winced in pain as he unwrapped his dirty bandage revealing the festering gunshot wound.

Will removed his small medicine bundle from his belt and took out some herbs. Then he stood up and walked over to Tiger.

"Let me see your wound," demanded Will.

9

The Escape

Too weak to put up a fight, Tiger held out his arm and allowed Will to treat his wound with the herbs.

"Why do you help me?" Tiger asked, roughly pulling his arm away as Will finished rewrapping the bandage.

"We are one people who have shared the sacred fire," answered Will quietly. "Seminoles help each other."

"But you are part white, and white blood has no honor," declared Tiger.

At that moment, the powerful voice of Osceola rang out from across the room. "Though I do not often speak of it," said the *tus-te-nug-gee,* "I am of mixed blood. Do you doubt my honor or my faithfulness to Seminole teachings?"

A look of shock crossed Tiger's face and he shrank back in shame at the words he had so carelessly uttered.

"I have friends among the white soldiers," continued the war chief. "Lieutenant John Graham is one of them. I have respect for him, as he does for me. My fight is not with individual white men, but with the U.S. government who forces us from our land."

Will stared at Osceola, trying to make sense of the war chief's words. As the meaning of his hero's revelation sank in, Will bowed respectfully to Osceola to show his gratitude. Then he walked back to his straw mat and lay down to ponder Osceola's startling disclosure. At that moment John Cypress's lesson came back to him.

A man should be judged by the way he lives his life, not by the color of his skin.

Will knew Tiger disliked him because he looked like the hated white man. It had taken the harsh words of Osceola to humble the quarrelsome brave. Perhaps now Tiger would understand the teaching of John Cypress and stop calling him "Half-blood."

With that hopeful thought, Will drifted off into a peaceful sleep.

Suddenly he was jolted awake by a hand covering his mouth. A commanding voice whispered in his ear. "Do not make a sound!"

"If you still have your knife, bury it," demanded the warrior. "Then pull your bedding back over the hole."

"Why?" asked Will softly, reaching for the knife that he had smuggled into the cell.

"Just do as I say. I am Wildcat."

Will shivered and nodded. He knew Wildcat was a powerful leader and warrior and the son of King Philip, so he followed Wildcat's instructions. Then he went back to sleep.

The next morning a guard opened the cell door and entered the dismal room. The prisoners watched in silence as he checked each one of them for hatchets and knives. Wildcat stood defiantly while the guard searched him. A smirk of satisfaction played at the warrior's lips when the guard found no weapons anywhere.

Little by little the Seminoles adjusted to their grim surroundings. Every morning the guard unlocked the door and brought in food and water. He tried to talk with them, but the Seminoles kept their distance. They would never trust a white man again.

As the days went by, Will regularly checked Tiger's wound. Slowly it improved, and so did the relationship between them. Tiger seemed more subdued and less of a bully since Osceola's reprimand. Will noticed Tiger's change of heart and he began to talk to Tiger each time he examined his arm.

"You are better," observed Will one November afternoon.

"John Cypress has taught you well," said Tiger. "I am grateful . . . and ashamed. I have given a lot of thought to what Osceola said. When I teased you, it made me feel important, but I was wrong. If I had looked beyond the color of your skin and eyes, I would have seen a true Seminole. I would be proud to call you my friend, Will Cypress."

Will was surprised Tiger admitted his mistakes and offered his friendship so freely. With the many grievances between them, it would be hard to build a friendship, but Tiger's attempt to make amends was a beginning. With a nod of his head Will accepted Tiger's apology and agreed to try.

As the month of November moved slowly toward December, boredom and the close living conditions of the cell forced the prisoners into frequent conversations. Will and Tiger had shared many experiences as children in the Snake Clan and now found that reliving some of those moments made the time go more quickly. Will and Tiger learned they had much in common and their friendship grew as the trust between them increased.

"We spent so much time making our first canoes," said Tiger.

"We worked together then," said Will, "to chop down the cypress trees and cut them in half. You showed me how to burn the middle with an ember from the campfire to soften the wood. Then we carved out the center with a stone."

"They were sturdy dugouts," said Tiger. "You used that canoe on your first alligator hunt with Samuel Carson."

"It pleased my father," said Will. "I was puffed up with pride."

"I was the same when I went off to join Osceola," said Tiger. "We both acted like boys. Now it's time give up our childish ways and work together against the white man."

"How do I know I can depend on you?" asked Will. "Angry words have passed between us."

"We will make a pact to stand as one against the enemy," said Tiger.

He removed a white egret feather from the leather pouch at his waist.

"I received this at my naming ceremony when I became a man. I give it to you with my word as a Seminole warrior that I will stand beside you in any fight that comes."

Will heard the depth of sincerity in Tiger's voice and believed him. He took the feather from Tiger's outstretched hand. Then Will reached up into his turban and pulled out the hawk feather that Billie had given him and handed it to Tiger.

"Our friendship is forever sealed," said Will.

* * *

One night Wildcat called a meeting. He suggested the prisoners try to remove the two iron bars from the high narrow window. Each night after that John Cavallo, a tall leader of the Black Seminoles, would stand below the window and allow warriors to take turns climbing onto his shoulders. Then each man would insert a knife blade between the stone bricks and, using the knife's handle for support, would crawl up to the ledge beneath the small opening. The warriors worked to loosen the iron bars, which were mounted in the brittle coquina stone.

Tiger's arm was still too sore for him to climb, so he stood watch when Will's turn came. After the guard left to make his nightly rounds, Tiger signaled with a low whistle. Quickly Will jumped on John's sturdy shoulders and hoisted himself up to the window. Will examined the iron bars and found one of them had already been bent.

Will gripped the straight bar with both hands. He angrily rocked it back and forth with all his strength. Suddenly he felt the coquina crumble and the bar give way. With one last mighty jerk, it broke loose!

Will held the bar up for the other warriors to see. Then he placed it back in the window so as not to arouse the suspicion of the guards. Removing the bar raised the spirits of the captives and gave them new hope that they might eventually escape.

As the days passed, Will noticed Osceola's health was rapidly failing and he worried about the war chief. He offered to treat him with herbs from the small medicine bundle John Cypress had given him, but Osceola told him Seminoles had little medicine against the white man's disease of malaria. The *tus-te-nug-gee* seemed resigned to his fate. Many times Wildcat asked Osceola to join in the escape plans, but he always refused that offer too.

Will often felt suffocated in the crowded cell and he would pace back and forth in the confined area like a caged animal. He missed running through the Florida wilderness and longed for the beauty of the Everglades. One day as he walked past Osceola, the war chief sat up and spoke to him.

"I have watched you become friends with Tiger," said Osceola. "You chose to show him respect even when it was not returned."

"It has been a hard lesson for me," said Will.

"It is a wise lesson," said the war chief. "If Seminoles and white men respected each other, there would be no war."

Will wanted to hear more from the war chief, but even those few words seemed to tire Osceola and he lay back down. Will left him to rest and went back to his straw mat. He removed the medicine bundle from his belt and took out the small crescent. As he ran his fingers over the polished metal, he remembered the day he had received it for rescuing his friend, Little Orchid. He thought about the day he had given the gorget in friendship to Zeke. He wondered again why Zeke had returned only one part of the necklace.

After a few minutes, Will placed the crescent back into the medicine bundle and joined the others planning the escape. Wildcat was talking when Will sat down.

"One bar has been removed. Now we can escape through that narrow opening," whispered Wildcat. "It is five feet high, but only eight inches wide. We must starve ourselves to lose weight so we can get through the window."

"In the meantime, we will make a long rope," continued Wildcat. "At the dark of the moon, I will tie it on the bent bar and throw it out the window. Then each of us will climb to the window, squeeze through, and slide down the rope to the moat below."

That night the prisoners tore their sacks into long strips. They braided the cloth into rope and hid it under the straw so the guards wouldn't see it. The captives passed the days starving themselves to lose weight and sleeping to conserve their strength. At night they worked on their rope and watched the moon through the window as it slowly waned.

Late one night, Wildcat explained his battle plan.

"Escape to the Everglades," he said. "Take your weapons

with you and go to the swamps near Lake Okeechobee. There we will make a stand and fight the U.S. army. We will not be tricked again!"

The next evening, Will, Tiger, and Charlie sat together talking quietly while they worked on their rope. They were very thin and counting the days until the dark of the moon.

"When we escape, we go south to fight at Lake Okeechobee alongside members of our own clan," said Charlie.

"We will warn the women and children to hide deeper in the Everglades," said Will, "where they will be safe from the bullets."

"Will knows how to use a rifle," said Tiger, "but he must learn the Seminole ways of bush fighting that Osceola taught us."

Then Tiger explained to Will how to put a notch in a tree to steady his gun and carry ammunition in his mouth during a battle. Tiger softly demonstrated the frightening war cry Osceola used when he attacked. He talked about the importance of posting lookouts in moss-covered trees to watch for soldiers and report their whereabouts to warriors on the ground.

"The swamps will work in our favor. We know the land and the heat does not bother us," said Tiger. "The soldiers foolishly wear heavy uniforms and advance in wide lines standing shoulder to shoulder. We attack from the trees and surprise them."

"I'm glad to learn these things before we fight," said Will.

One night no moonlight came through the window at the ceiling. All the prisoners pretended to sleep so the guard would leave them alone. When Wildcat thought it was safe, he took the braided rope from under the straw and slung it around his neck. Then he climbed onto John Cavallo's shoulders, inserted the blade of a knife between the rocks, and scaled the wall up to the window. He tied one end of the rope securely to the bent bar and threw it out the opening. The rope slapped against the thick outside wall of the fort.

The prisoners watched as Wildcat twisted his lean body through the narrow window. Will listened until he heard a quiet thump outside. Wildcat had escaped!

10

Will's Decision

One by one, eighteen Seminole braves and two squaws took turns climbing to the window and then disappearing through its tiny opening.

When it was time for the Snake Clan to go, Charlie escaped first. But when Tiger tried to climb on John Cavallo's shoulders, he fell back.

"My arm is still too weak," he said.

"You must try harder," encouraged Will. "Step into my hands and I will boost you up."

Tiger put one foot into Will's hands and Will lifted him to John Cavallo's shoulders. Tiger grimaced in pain as he pulled up to the window and squeezed through it. Will heard him groan as Tiger climbed down the outside wall and dropped to the ground.

Next it was Will's turn. He looked over at Osceola and acknowledged his hero with a slight lift of his hand. Osceola accepted Will's tribute with a solemn nod. Will would never forget the war chief's courage. Osceola had led his people bravely, but disease and betrayal had extinguished the fire of his passion. It was now up to Will and the other warriors to continue the fight.

Will climbed on John Cavallo's shoulders and pulled himself onto the window ledge. He could see nothing in the inky night, but Will confidently grabbed the rope. Holding his breath, he slid through the window and scaled down the rough shell bricks on the outside of the fort. When the rope ended, Will dropped into the muddy ditch below.

Tiger was waiting and helped Will to his feet. It felt good to be outside again in the open air. As he and Tiger crept away from the fort, Will vowed never to be captured again.

Wildcat, Charlie, and the other Seminoles had already melted into the palmettos outside the fort, traveling alone or in pairs so they would not attract the attention of the soldiers. Together, Will and Tiger started their journey south to Lake Okeechobee. They ate off the land, sharing what little food they could find, always keeping their eyes open for white soldiers.

One night as they slept in the thick branches of a live oak tree, Will and Tiger were awakened by the sound of galloping horses. Suddenly a group of U.S. army cavalrymen came crashing through the palmettos, their pistols drawn and ready to shoot.

Will and Tiger waited quietly as the line of soldiers thundered beneath them and disappeared in a cloud of dust. Then a lone cavalryman bringing up the rear galloped under the branches of the live oak tree. Tiger gave the piercing Seminole war cry and jumped down on the soldier's back, pulling him to the ground. Will followed and grabbed the soldier's rifle when it fell from the saddle into the dirt. As Tiger wrestled with the soldier, the black horse trotted off and stood nearby, snorting and pawing the ground. Suddenly the terrified man tore free from Tiger's grasp and ran into the palmetto underbrush. Will aimed his rifle at the bushes.

"Let him go," said Tiger. "He cannot hurt us now, and the sound of gunfire will attract attention. Get the horse. We must leave before the soldiers come back."

"With this gun, your hatchet, my knife, and a horse, we are warriors again!" said Will, jubilantly slinging the rifle over his shoulder so he could pat the nose of the stallion to calm him. "This animal is strong like a chief. His name will be Micco."

Tiger hurriedly pulled the soldier's saddle off Micco and he and Will rode bareback on the powerful black horse, trying to put distance between them and the soldiers. To give Micco a rest, they walked on foot along the path that bordered the St. Johns River. Sometimes they traveled in the shallow water near the banks, always watching for cottonmouth moccasins that lurked among the tall reeds. Once Micco reared on his hind legs and snorted loudly, warning them of an alligator that lay half submerged in the muddy river.

"He is a good horse," said Will, stroking Micco's mane. "The Breath Maker smiled on us that night the soldiers rode under our tree."

When the sun was high, they followed a small stream that meandered off the St. Johns into the woods. Will tied Micco to a tree to graze while Tiger took a flint from his pouch and started a fire. Then Will hiked deeper into the pine flatwoods to hunt for small game.

It didn't take long for Will to shoot three squirrels and skin them. He brought them back to the fire and placed them on a stick for roasting. While the meat cooked, he and Tiger went back into the woods to look for fruit and berries. When they came upon a wild orange tree, they stopped and picked as many of the citrus fruits as they could carry. With their arms full of oranges, the two started back to the campfire.

Suddenly Will spotted a short cabbage palm tree.

Knowing the tender heart of the palm would be a tasty addition to their meal, he raced toward it. As Will ran, the oranges spilled from his arms and rolled in all directions. He stopped and started picking up the fruit from the underbrush.

As Will reached for an orange half-hidden in a mound of pine needles, he heard the ominous warning of a diamondback rattlesnake curled and poised to strike. He froze in his place anticipating the poisonous bite. At that moment Will felt a rush of air as Tiger's hatchet flew past his ear. Its sharp blade struck with a deadly aim and killed the viper with one blow. The head of the rattlesnake lay beside the tail that continued to writhe and shake its rattles with the foreboding sound that caused fear in the heart of even the bravest of men.

Will stood up and backed away from the dying snake. He took several deep breaths to calm his rapid heartbeat. Tiger ran up behind him and grabbed his shoulder.

"You are all right?" he asked.

"I'm safe because of your swift action," said Will. "*Sho-nah-beh-sha*. Thank you."

"You are my Seminole brother," said Tiger. "We have a pact to protect each other."

"I hope the cabbage is worth the trouble," said Will with a smile.

"We have no pot to boil it in, but even uncooked cabbage will fill our hungry stomachs," responded Tiger.

Then Tiger picked up his hatchet and began chopping down the cabbage palm tree. When he finished, Will cut stalks from the heart of the palm with his knife and the two started back to camp, gathering the scattered oranges as they went.

The smell of roasting meat wafted through the woods, enticing the two famished braves to hurry. When they arrived back at the fire, Will walked over to Micco who was still quietly grazing and offered him a peeled orange. The horse's prickly tongue tickled Will's flattened hand as Micco lapped up the fruit and licked the juice that dripped from his fingers. Will left another orange on the ground for Micco to finish and then joined Tiger at the fire to eat his own meal.

After the meager rations at Osceola's camp and Fort Marion, the meal seemed like a feast. It was the most they had eaten since leaving the prison and their full stomachs made them sleepy. The two were tempted to remain there for the night, but following a short rest, Will untied Micco and he and Tiger climbed on the stallion's back to continue the journey toward Lake Okeechobee.

As the warriors moved down the Florida peninsula, Will thought often about what lay ahead. He knew fierce fighting would come, but Tiger had taught him well and he was ready. Will thought about the great courage it would take to face the white man in battle and he felt confident knowing Tiger would fight beside him. He absentmindedly reached for the gorget he had been given for courage in helping his friend, Little Orchid. When he remembered he had given the necklace to Zeke, he slowed his pace and took out the small crescent from his medicine bundle. He again wondered what would happen to Zeke and the boys during the war. He tried to push the questions about their welfare to the back of his mind.

Suddenly his thoughts came together like pieces of a puzzle.

"Tiger, stop!" Will called to his friend who was ahead of him scouting for game.

"What's wrong?" called Tiger as he walked over to Will and Micco.

"I must go back," said Will.

"Why?" asked Tiger. "The white soldiers are close behind us. We must get to Lake Okeechobee."

Will began to unravel the story of finding his half-sister and her three children. He related the sequence of events in detail, trying to make Tiger understand.

"On my way to Osceola's camp, I stumbled onto a farmhouse in the woods. I was weak with hunger and the white widow living there gave me food. She was raising her three boys alone and was very sick.

"My blue eyes and ability to speak English," continued Will, "convinced her I was the half-brother she had been searching for. It seemed unbelievable. My father never told me I had a sister. But she had proof in a locket that held Samuel Carson's image. She asked me to stay with them at the farm, but I wanted to join Osceola."

"I got along well with her two younger boys, but her oldest son, Zeke, did not like me. I tried to show him friendship by giving him my silver gorget."

Tiger looked confused as he listened. Then Will pulled out the silver crescent Zeke had left with Osceola.

"Zeke risked his life to return one crescent of the gorget to me. It is only half of the necklace," continued Will. "I think it is an offer of *his* friendship and a plea for help. I must answer such a request."

"It is a strange path you choose," said Tiger. "We are warriors and our destiny is to fight the white man, not help him."

"As a boy it was my dream to become a Seminole warrior," said Will, "but the return of the gorget has changed everything. My heart beats with two bloods that call me. I will bring honor to both if I return to help my sister's children as John Cypress taught me."

"I promised I would stand beside you in any fight that came," said Tiger. "I cannot enter the battle in your heart, my friend, but I will stand beside your decision."

"When you see my uncle, tell him what I am doing," said Will.

"You have my word," replied Tiger. "John Cypress will be proud that you have honored his teachings."

"And when you see Little Orchid," added Will, "tell her to look for me at next year's Green Corn Dance."

"I will," promised Tiger.

Will reached out and grasped Tiger's shoulder firmly.

"Take the rifle," said Will, handing Tiger the gun. Then he added, "May the Breath Maker protect you in battle so that we may meet again."

"You take Micco," said Tiger. "He will carry you swiftly to your nephews. Then may the Breath Maker safely guide your footsteps."

"Goodbye, my friend," said Will. "We have traveled many paths together. Now we must go our separate ways. I follow the road to the white world, but I will never forget you or the teachings of my Seminole life."

Then Will took Micco's reins from Tiger's outstretched hands and jumped on the horse's back. The black stallion sensed the urgency in Will's touch and seemed to read his thoughts. With no signal from Will, Micco started running north toward the path to Mary's house.

Like Will, Micco loved running and the pair flew like the wind through the pine flatwoods, jumping over streams and fallen trees. Will stopped to rest only when Micco needed to graze or drink from a stream. Then he would find some fruit or berries for himself and stretch out on the ground for a short nap. In two days' time Will reached the dusty path that led to Mary's house. He left Micco tied to a tree and cautiously approached on foot, fearing the worst for Zeke and his brothers.

When the farmhouse came into view, Will could see Zeke sitting on the porch cleaning the gun that rested across his legs. Robert was coming around the side of the house holding Sam's hand. When Robert saw Will walking up the lane, he picked up his little brother and began running toward him.

"Will, you've come back," he shouted. "You've come back!"

Zeke looked up from his task, and seeing his uncle, immediately dashed down the porch steps. When the four came together in the middle of the yard they stood awkwardly for a moment, not knowing what to say to each other. Finally Zeke spoke.

11

Becoming a Carson

"I knew you would come," Zeke said, gratitude shining in his eyes. Will was pleased to see that half of the silver necklace he had given to Zeke hung around the boy's neck.

"I was not sure of your meaning when you returned one piece of the gorget," said Will, pulling out the matching silver crescent.

"I left it as a sign of my friendship," said Zeke. "I wasn't sure what I should tell the Seminoles, but I hoped you would understand that I wanted you to come back."

Will reached out and began to tie the crescent back onto Zeke's necklace.

"That is what I thought," he said. "Now like us, the gorget is together again."

"We've tried to keep up with the chores, but it's been hard," said Robert, setting Sam on the ground. "I've had to take care of Sam and even wash his clothes when he soiled his pants. Yuck!"

Will felt a tug on the strings of his leggings and looked down. He smiled as he bent over and picked up his little nephew who was dressed in a pair of ragged overalls.

"Let's sit on the porch and talk," said Will. "You have a lot to tell me."

The boys settled on the floor around Will and told him of their troubled days since their mother had died.

"Ma got so sick and she was coughing all the time. Finally she took to her bed," said Zeke. "I gave her medicine, but it didn't seem to help.

"Just before Ma died, she called me over to her bedside. She told me that she had sent a letter to Pa's brother, Henry Whitney, asking him to come here. She said Uncle Henry was a good man and she was sure he would take care of us. Every day she looked out of the window, expecting him to ride up the lane.

"After Ma died," continued Zeke, "I tried to find you, Will, but you were not at Osceola's camp, so I left part of the gorget and the message. Then I came home to wait for Uncle Henry. Because Ma seemed so certain he would come, we boys just stayed on here and did the best we could while we waited."

"But Uncle Henry never came," said Robert sadly. Then, brightening, he added, "But *you* came, Will!"

"Yes, I came," said Will. "Maybe your other uncle did not receive Mary's letter. It is wartime."

"Will is right," agreed Robert. "Uncle Henry never met us, but he always enclosed funny sketches for us in the letters he sent to Pa. That shows he was thinking about us, doesn't it?"

"Yes," said Will. "He would not draw pictures to amuse you if he didn't care. Do you know where Henry Whitney lives?"

"I'm not sure," said Zeke, "but Pa saved his brother's letters and kept them in a box somewhere in Ma's desk. Maybe Uncle Henry's address is on one of the envelopes."

"Find the letters, Zeke," said Will. "I'll put my horse in the barn while you look."

"You have a horse, Will?" asked Robert. His eyes widened with interest.

"Yes," answered Will. "Bring Sam and come with me to meet him."

As Robert and Sam left with Will, Zeke went inside the farmhouse and searched his mother's old pine desk. In a few minutes he came back with a small rectangular box. He sat down and began going through the papers inside it. At last he pulled out a stack of letters tied with a string.

"Here's one from Uncle Henry," called Zeke as Will and the two younger boys came back to the porch. "It's from Savannah, Georgia."

"Good," said Will. "Tomorrow I will ride to the trading post and learn the way to Savannah."

Zeke nodded and continued looking through the contents of the box.

"Here's the paper that shows we own this place," he said. "What should we do with it?"

"I'll take it with me. Someone at the trading post may want to buy the farm," said Will.

When Zeke came upon Mary's oval locket in the box, he took it out and held it up to the light for a moment. Then with a sigh he dropped the necklace into the box and went inside to put it back in the drawer of the old desk.

When he returned, Will said, "Write down supplies we need. I will get them at the trading post. I will borrow your pa's clothes and dress like a white man to go into the white man's territory."

"I know where his clothes are," said Robert. "Ma packed up Pa's things and put them under their bed."

He ran to get them, happy to be included in the adventure at last.

At sunrise the next morning Will cut his hair short and

covered it with Zeke Whitney's wide-brimmed hat. He dressed in the faded shirt and pants that Robert had given him. The clothes were too big so he stuffed the shirttail inside the pants and used a piece of rope as a belt. Then Will pulled on the man's old leather boots and worn overcoat. He stepped outside into the December chill and headed toward the barn to get Micco. When he jumped on the stallion's back, the horse seemed to sense his master's wish for speed. Micco's step never faltered as the two raced as one toward the trading post.

When Will reached the store, he left Micco tied to the railing out front and went inside the small building. He pulled his hat further down over his face and tried to walk confidently in the borrowed boots. A lone man stood behind the counter.

"Mornin'," the proprietor said, looking Will up and down suspiciously. "I don't think I've seen you around these parts. What's your name?"

Will raised his head to look the man in the eye. "I am Mary Whitney's brother . . . uh, uh, Will Carson," he stammered. He had never spoken the name before and it sounded strange to his ears.

"I heard she passed on, but I never heard mention of any brother," said the man scratching his chin thoughtfully. "There's something about you that looks a little different. Are you really her kin?"

"Here is my proof," said Will, handing him the deed to the farm. "Mary Whitney's boys want to sell the land. They will live with relatives in Savannah."

"They're too young to handle that farm for sure. I reckon I could take it off your hands for twenty-five dollars for them fifty acres right now," said the man, looking up from the document, "including the farmhouse and the livestock, of course."

Will did not know the value of the white man's money, but he knew the boys needed whatever they could get. He nodded his agreement to the man's offer. The proprietor quickly printed some words on the bottom of the paper and slid it across the counter to Will.

"I cannot read," said Will. "What does it say?"

"Don't you trust me?" asked the man angrily, bringing his gun up from under the counter and laying it in plain view.

Will started to edge slowly backwards toward the door. As he reached for the doorknob, the man hollered, "Come back! I'll give you thirty dollars. Just put your mark right here where it says 'Sold to Silas P. Bagwell on December 18, 1837.'"

Will walked to the counter and picked up the storekeeper's pencil. Then he made an X on the spot where the man's dirty fingernail pointed.

As Silas Bagwell counted out the money, Will asked, "What is the best route to Savannah?"

"Takin' them there yourself, are you? I reckon you'll be safe enough if you follow the St. Johns River north from here. Most of the battles with them Seminoles are farther south near the Everglades. Stick to the shoreline of the Atlantic Ocean and you'll run right smack into Savannah."

The storekeeper handed Will the money and Will quickly stuck it in the pocket of his overcoat.

"Thank you," said Will. "Here is a list of supplies we need."

The proprietor took the piece of paper and began gathering the items together. While wrapping them in brown paper, the man sneaked several looks at Will as if still trying to figure out who he was. Finally he handed Will the bundle.

"No charge," said the man. "Them boys deserve a break

what with the death of their ma and all."

"Thank you," said Will, taking the package. "We will be leaving the farm the day after tomorrow."

"I'll send my son over to care for the livestock after you leave," said the proprietor. "I assume you'll be takin' the Whitney's horse to carry your supplies?"

Will nodded to the man and then hurriedly strode out of the trading post. As he mounted Micco and started back, the gold coins jingled in Zeke Whitney's coat pocket, reminding Will of the deal he had struck with Silas Bagwell. He worried about it some, but figured he had done the best he could. Mostly Will was just relieved to have his business with the white man finished. He knew his ordeal was finally over when he turned onto the dirt road that led to Mary's house and saw the welcoming glow of Zeke's lantern in the front window of the farmhouse.

The next morning Will gave Zeke the gold from the sale of the farm.

"When we get to Savannah, Zeke, give it to your uncle."

"That's a good idea, Will," said Zeke. Then he laughed and added, "I bet Uncle Henry will like that idea, too!"

The rest of the day the boys prepared to leave the farm. Will and Zeke fed the animals and cleaned the barn. Robert stayed in the house, keeping an eye on Sam and packing their few belongings. That night they ate the supper of ham and beans that Robert fixed. After setting some cornbread aside for breakfast, the rest of the food was packed for the trip. The boys were exhausted from the day's work and gratefully climbed into their cots for their final night at the farmhouse. In a few minutes Will heard the boys' soft snoring and he slipped out to the shed to sleep in the open air.

Before the sun rose the next day Will was loading

supplies onto Micco and the farm horse, Dolly. As dawn broke over the horizon, he went to the porch and called the boys to come outside. Robert brought out breakfast and the four ate in silence, dipping their cornbread in cups of milk.

When they finished their meal, Will said, "Bring the left-over cornbread with two cups of milk and follow me."

"Why?" Robert asked.

"We will leave the cornbread and milk at your parents' graves," explained Will. "Seminoles leave food and drink for eating in the afterlife."

"What else do they do?" asked Zeke, as Robert went into the house.

"We bury things they used with them," answered Will. "We believe our people will need their tools."

"I'll be right back," said Zeke, following Robert inside.

When the boys returned, Zeke had Mary's gold necklace and his Pa's harmonica in his hands. Robert carried two cups of milk carefully balanced on top of the skillet of cornbread. Then Will took Sam's hand and led his three nephews to the graves of Mary and Zeke Whitney in the small cemetery behind the farm.

"Leave the milk and bread here," said Will, pointing to a spot in front of the two wooden crosses. "Break off those palmetto branches and cover the food with them."

Then Will began digging a small hole between the graves.

When he finished, he said, "You must break the chain and harmonica before you bury them. The spirit inside will go to the Hereafter too."

Zeke did as he was directed and solemnly set the items in the small pocket Will had scooped in the earth. Then Zeke took his younger brothers' hands and bowed his head as Will covered the locket and harmonica with dirt.

"Bow your heads, too," Zeke whispered to Robert and Sam.

Then he began his prayer. "Heavenly Father, we know Ma and Pa are angels up there with you. Tell them Will is taking us to Uncle Henry's and not to worry."

"And tell them we love them," added Robert. "They were good parents and didn't mean to leave us alone. Amen."

"Amen," echoed Zeke softly.

The boys quietly followed Will in single file back to the barn, stepping in each other's footprints as they went.

Robert looked up at his Seminole uncle and asked, "Will, if you're here with us, do we really have to leave?"

12

Friends Forever

Will silently scanned each boy's face as he considered Robert's request to stay at the farm. At times he'd had the same thought himself, but in his heart he knew it would be impossible for him to raise three boys alone. They would be better off with a mother and father to care for them.

"Robert, we must go to Savannah," answered Will. "Your family there can take better care of you."

Then hoping to distract Robert a little, he added, "Would you like to ride Micco today?"

A broad grin spread across Robert's face and he ran into the barn. In a minute he came out riding Micco and leading Dolly. Will climbed up on Dolly's wide back and stretched out his hands for Zeke to hand Sam up to him. He sat his youngest nephew in front of him and waited while Zeke stood on a bucket and jumped up behind Robert.

As they rode side by side down the farm's lane for the last time, Will glanced at the sad young faces of Zeke and Robert. Even Sam stopped squirming and leaned his small body against Will for comfort. For a while the group traveled without saying a word. Will understood the boys' reluctance to leave the only place they had ever called home. He remembered having that same hollow feeling when his clan fled from the reservation.

Their horses kept a steady pace through the forest for several hours. As the heavy morning mist lifted so did their spirits, and the grief-stricken look finally disappeared from the boys' eyes. When they reached the St. Johns River, they dismounted to stretch their legs and eat some of the food they'd packed.

While they ate, Robert said, "I feel better, Will. You can ride Micco from now on. He really likes you best."

Will smiled and patted Micco's long nose as the horse nuzzled his shirt. Then the four mounted again and continued their journey along the river, always on the lookout for danger. Whenever they met strangers, Will would wave and keep riding. He was suspicious of white men and only spoke to them when absolutely necessary. When they reached the mouth of the St. Johns River, Will skirted around the port town of Jacksonville.

Will and the boys traveled until they saw the mighty Atlantic Ocean, rolling onto shore with huge white-capped waves. Once they were on the beige-colored sand, Will threw caution aside and let the horses gallop freely by the water's edge. Their hooves sent sprays of cold water over the riders, but no one minded. The four laughed and shouted with joy because it felt good to race the wind. That night they rolled up in their blankets and slept on the beach under the stars.

As they crossed into Georgia, Will became more cautious. He was nervous traveling through the open marshland and longed for the protective trees and underbrush of the Everglades.

It was late in the day when they finally entered the city of Savannah. A cold evening wind blowing off the river whipped around them. As they rode down the cobblestone street, Will and the boys stared in wonder. Men were loading tall sailing ships with cotton bales from the multi-storied warehouses that lined the waterfront. Zeke stopped Dolly near a man working on the docks to ask directions to his uncle's house.

"It's just two streets over," said the man, pointing to the left. "It's not far at all."

Zeke thanked the man, and he and Will turned the horses inland toward the lights of the city. A light snow was falling and under the street lamps, the snowflakes turned into flecks of pure gold. Little Sam stuck out his tongue to catch the falling flakes and Zeke and Robert caught them on the palms of their hands.

"What do you call this cold rain?" asked Will, brushing snowflakes from Micco's mane. "I've never seen it before."

"It's snow," said Zeke. "Ma told me about it. She said she wanted to live in Florida because it never got cold enough to snow. Ma liked to be warm."

The snow amazed the four, but nothing had prepared Will and the boys for the sights of Savannah. Horse-drawn carriages rolled up and down streets built around large public squares where gardens grew. The beautiful quadrangles were surrounded by stately brick homes with huge live oak trees in the yards.

At last, they found Henry Whitney's house. The three-story home was built of gray brick and had two white columns framing the doorway. Wreaths of holly hung in the windows giving the house a festive air.

Zeke took out his uncle's letter and checked the street address. It matched the numbers on the house, so he and Robert climbed down off Dolly. Will handed Sam down to Robert and then he too dismounted. After tying the horses to the gatepost, the four travelers walked hesitantly up the stone walkway. As they drew closer, they could hear the sound of singing drifting out from the windows.

"That's 'Silent Night,'" cried Robert. "It must be Christmas!"

Will stood with Robert and Sam while Zeke went alone up the front steps and stood on the porch landing. Zeke squared his shoulders and took a deep breath. Then he knocked firmly on the door. A middle-aged man dressed in a green silk coat opened it and stepped out onto the landing. Behind the man, Will could see a family silhouetted by candlelight. Two girls and a boy were singing with a lady sitting by a large evergreen tree.

"Uncle Henry?" asked Zeke timidly. "I'm Zeke Whitney, your nephew." Then he turned and pointed. "And over there is Robert and Sam and Ma's brother, Will."

The tall man carefully studied Zeke's face through his gold-rimmed glasses.

"Well, this is certainly a pleasant surprise!" he said. "I had no idea you were coming here for Christmas and all the way from Florida, too. Where is your mother?"

Zeke's voice cracked when he spoke and his bottom lip began to quiver. "You didn't get the letter Ma sent you about us?"

"Why no, Zeke, I never received a letter," said the man. "Is something wrong?"

"Ma died in October," blurted Zeke. "Before she passed on, she wrote asking you to come to Florida to help us. She was so sure you would come . . ."

Henry Whitney leaned down and put his hands on Zeke's trembling shoulders.

"I'm so sorry, Zeke," said the man. "I didn't know about your mother or your troubles. Come right in and we'll sort all this out."

Then Henry Whitney straightened up and called, "Come in everyone and get warm by the fire."

Robert picked up Sam and followed Zeke and Uncle Henry into the living room where a warm fire crackled in the fireplace and the sweet smells of Christmas pudding and cinnamon cookies filled the air.

As the boys warmed their hands, Uncle Henry continued, "If I had received the letter, boys, I would have come directly to Florida. But don't worry anymore. There is a place for all of you in our home."

Then Uncle Henry began introducing them to their cousins and Aunt Clara. At that moment Zeke realized that Will had not come in with them so he went back outside to get him.

"You must come too," he pleaded, grabbing Will's hand and pulling him toward the door.

"Your white uncle will take care of you, Zeke," said Will. "It is as it should be. You and your brothers are safe now."

"But I want you to live with us, too," cried Zeke, tears beginning to stream down his cheeks. "Uncle Henry said there's plenty of room in this big house for all of us!"

"I'd like to stay with you forever," said Will, "but I cannot live in the white world. I need the wilderness of the Everglades. You have walked in my footsteps. Now you are ready to make your own path."

Will pointed to the silver necklace at Zeke's neck. "The gorget will remind you of our true friendship. When you wear it, remember that deep in the Everglades you have a Seminole uncle who will always care about you."

Zeke nodded bravely and tried to rub his tears away with the palm of his hand. As he stepped back onto the landing, Henry Whitney came and stood beside him, putting his arm around the boy's thin shoulders. Then Aunt Clara walked out holding Sam and Robert's hands and the rest of Henry Whitney's family crowded behind them in the doorway.

"You are welcome here too," Henry Whitney said to Will. "Won't you at least spend the night with us?"

"Thank you," said Will, "but it will be easier on the boys if I leave now."

Hearing Will's reply, Robert pulled away from Aunt Clara and ran down the steps. He latched onto Will's legs and hugged them hard. Sam toddled after Robert and ran to Will with his arms outstretched. Will picked up the little boy and then reached down and tousled Robert's hair the way he had seen Mary do.

Aunt Clara hurried to Will and took Sam from him in a practiced motherly fashion. Then she took Robert's hand and gently pulled him away.

Will looked gratefully into the kind woman's eyes and said, "You and your husband are good. My nephews will be happy here."

"Thank you for bringing them to us," replied Aunt Clara. "We will love and take care of these boys like they were our own."

As she walked Robert and Sam back to the porch, she whispered to the boys, "If Will wants to go, then we must let him. You are home now."

When they reached the landing, Henry Whitney gathered his wife and the children all together. Zeke stood between his two brothers, trying to look grown up as they all waved goodbye to Will.

"Zeke, you have taken good care of your family," called Will, jumping on Micco's back. "You would be a good Seminole."

Suddenly Micco reared up on his hind legs and pawed the air with his hooves. The horse's nostrils flared and his ears twitched nervously as if somewhere off in the distance he could hear the Snake Clan summoning them home. As the stallion's forefeet dropped to the ground, he lifted his black head high and pranced back and forth, eager to run with the wind. Then Will gave Micco a kick and the two galloped into the night to answer the irresistible call of the Everglades.

Historical Notes

Black Seminoles: African-American slaves who escaped from plantations in Alabama and Georgia and fled into Florida. They were welcomed by the Seminoles and fought side by side with them against the U.S. army in the Second Seminole War. Some were enslaved, but worked like tenant farmers who paid rent. Eventually many Black Seminoles bought their farms and set up villages, electing their own chiefs. Some married Seminoles and became part of Seminole families.

chickee: A Seminole house built on stilts. It has open sides and a palmetto-thatched roof.

clan: A group of families living in a Seminole village. Seminole children belong to their mother's clan. Names of the clans come from nature, for example, the Panther and the Snake Clans.

Coa Hadjo: A major leader and war chief in the Second Seminole War. He served as Osceola's interpreter and spoke for the Seminoles when they met with General Hernandez at Fort Peyton. He was captured under a white flag of truce and imprisoned in Fort Marion with Osceola.

coontie: The root of this plant is pounded into flour to make Seminole bread.

Florida Everglades: Approximately three million acres of water, swamps, hammocks, and marsh grass that lie below Lake Okeechobee. The Everglades extend about one hundred miles south to the tip of the Florida peninsula. It was called *Pa-hay-okee* by the Seminoles, which means "grassy water." The tall sawgrass and shallow water form a river that is the heart of the Everglades. Many types of animals, reptiles, insects, birds, air plants, flowers, and trees are found here. Everglades National Park is located on the southwestern tip of the Florida peninsula and is open year-round for visitors.

Fort Brooke: A military post on Tampa Bay established in 1824. During the Second Seminole War, the Seminoles and Black Seminoles were held at the fort. The Seminoles were waiting to be put on ships and sent to Indian Territory west of the Mississippi River (now Oklahoma). When Osceola learned that the Black Seminoles would be kept in Florida and likely be returned to slavery, he convinced the prisoners at the fort to escape to the Everglades.

Fort Marion (Castillo de San Marcos): Built of coquina blocks between 1672 and 1695 to guard St. Augustine. The old fort, called Fort Marion during the Second Seminole War, was used by the U.S. Army. In 1837, Osceola was captured under the white flag of truce and imprisoned here. Today, Castillo de San Marcos is part of the National Park System and visitors can tour the historic fortress and grounds.

Fort Peyton: This fort, about ten miles south of St. Augustine, was established during the Second Seminole War. The soldiers who captured Osceola in October of 1837 were housed here.

General Joseph Hernandez: A Spanish Floridian born in St. Augustine. He shared public disgrace with General Jesup for capturing Osceola under the white flag of truce near Fort Peyton. He failed to win a seat in the U.S. Senate in 1845 and moved to Cuba where he died in 1857.

General Thomas Jesup: The commander of the U.S. Army in the Second Seminole War. In October of 1837 General Jesup ordered General Hernandez to ignore the white flag of truce and capture Osceola and Coa Hadjo when they came to a council meeting near Fort Peyton. Many white Americans began to sympathize with the plight of the Seminole people when they learned of his treachery.

gorget (gor'jit): A crescent-shaped necklace worn by Seminole men.

Green Corn Dance: An annual four-day festival celebrated for the general health and well-being of the Seminole people. It is a time to socialize with friends and conduct tribal politics. A court is held to administer justice for serious crimes.

Indian reservation: Land set aside by the U.S. government for use by the Indians. In Florida, there are six Seminole reservations. They are the Tampa, Brighton, Immokalee, Big Cypress, Fort Pierce, and Hollywood Reservations. There is also a Seminole reservation in Oklahoma.

John Cavallo: A Black Seminole chief who was known for his courage, intelligence, and excellent marksmanship. He escaped from Fort Marion with Wildcat and commanded African-American warriors at the Battle of Lake Okeechobee. He was deported to the Indian Territory in 1838, but later led a group of Black Seminoles into Mexico, where he started a settlement of freed men.

King Philip: A Seminole leader and the father of Wildcat. He was captured with his son near St. Augustine in September 1837 by General Hernandez and imprisoned in Ft. Marion. Wildcat escaped, but King Philip remained a prisoner.

Lieutenant John Graham: A friend and companion of the war chief Osceola. There is a story that Osceola told his warriors to spare Graham's life at the Battle of the Withlacoochee.

micco: A word meaning "chief" in the Seminole language.

Osceola (1804–1838): A Seminole war chief during the Second Seminole War. When U.S. soldiers attempted to remove all Seminoles to Indian Territory in the west, Osceola, whose name means "black drink crier," refused to leave his Florida homeland. He recruited and trained Seminoles to fight against the U.S. Army. Osceola led warriors on fierce raids, ambushing U.S. soldiers and then disappearing into the swamps. In 1836, Osceola fell ill with malaria and in 1837 he was captured and imprisoned in Fort Marion at St. Augustine, Florida. Later he was transported to Fort Moultrie at Charleston, South Carolina, where he died in January 1838.

Pa-hay-okee: A word meaning "grassy water" in the Seminole language.

Second Seminole War: This war (1835–1842) was the longest and most costly of all the Indian Wars in the United States. When land-hungry white settlers started moving into Florida, they wanted to settle on Seminole land. The issue of slavery also caused conflicts between the white men and the Indians. Alabama and Georgia slaves crossed into Florida seeking freedom. The Seminoles took runaway slaves into their villages and protected them from slave catchers. In 1830, President Andrew Jackson signed the Indian Removal Act. In exchange for desirable land east of the Mississippi River, Indians would move west of the Mississippi River to Indian Territory, which is now the state of Oklahoma. Some Seminoles refused to leave their Florida homeland. When the U.S. Army came to Florida to remove them, the Seminole warriors, lead by war chief Osceola, fought back. In December 1835, the war began with three separate Indian attacks against the U.S. Army. The fighting continued for seven years. Finally, most of the Seminoles surrendered and were shipped west to Indian Territory.

Seminoles: Descendants of the Muskogee or Creek Indians from Georgia and Alabama. To escape from white settlers who were taking over the land during the 1700s, this group of Creeks moved to northern Florida. They were called "Seminoles," which means "runaway" or "free people" because they preferred to live away from white men. The Seminoles never signed a peace treaty with the U.S. government. A few Seminoles escaped to the Everglades where their descendants still live today.

sofkee: A thin corn soup of the Seminoles.

tus-te-nug-gee: A word meaning "war chief" in the Seminole language.

U.S. Army: Soldiers sent by the U.S. government to protect the white settlers in Florida and to force Seminoles to move west. The U.S. cavalry, a branch of the army, was made up of soldiers who fought on horseback.

Wildcat: Considered the ablest of the Indian leaders by General Jesup. His father was King Philip. Wildcat had ambitions of succeeding his uncle, Chief Micanopy, as head chief of the Seminoles. Handsome and athletic, he was in his twenties when war broke out. Stories are told of his stopping to laugh at soldiers chasing him and then easily outrunning them. When Wildcat escaped from Fort Marion, he went south to lead the Seminoles at the Battle of Lake Okeechobee. It was the largest battle of the Second Seminole War and occurred on Christmas Day, 1837. Eventually Wildcat was also sent to the Indian Territory. Like his friend, John Cavallo, he left the Territory and went to live in Mexico, where he died of smallpox in 1857.

Here are some other books from Pineapple Press on related topics. For a complete catalog, write to Pineapple Press, P.O. Box 3889, Sarasota, Florida 34230-3889, or call (800) 746-3275. Or visit our website at www.pineapplepress.com.

Escape to the Everglades Teacher's Activity Guide by Edwina Raffa and Annelle Rigsby. The authors of *Escape to the Everglades* have written a teacher's manual filled with activities to help students learn more about Florida and the Seminoles. Includes references to the Sunshine State Standards. (pb)

Kidnapped in Key West by Edwina Raffa and Annelle Rigsby. Twelve-year-old Eddie Malone is living a carefree life swimming and fishing in the Florida Keys in 1912 when suddenly his world is turned upside down. His father, a worker on Henry Flagler's Over-Sea Railroad, is thrown into jail for stealing the railroad payroll. Eddie sets out for Key West with his faithful dog, Rex, on a daring mission to prove his father's innocence. Eddie finds the real thieves, but they kidnap him and lock him aboard their sailboat. As the boat moves swiftly away from Key West, Eddie realizes he's in serious trouble. Can he escape their clutches in time to foil the thieves' next plot and prove his pa's innocence? (hb) Teacher's Activity Guide is also available with activities to help students learn more about Key West and Flagler's Over-Sea Railroad. Includes references to the Sunshine State Standards. (pb)

The Treasure of Amelia Island by M.C. Finotti. These are the ruminations of Mary Kingsley, the youngest child of former slave Ana Jai Kingsley, as she recounts the life-changing events of December 1813. Her family lived in La Florida, a Spanish territory under siege by Patriots who see no place for freed people of color in a new Florida. Against these mighty events, Mary decides to search for a legendary pirate treasure with her brothers. This treasure hunt, filled with danger and recklessness, changes Mary forever. (hb)

Blood Moon Rider by Zack C. Waters. When his Marine father is killed in WWII, young Harley Wallace is exiled to the Florida cattle ranch of his grandfather. The murder of a cowman and the disappearance of Grandfather Wallace leads Harley and his new friend Beth on a wild ride through the swamps and into the midst of a conspiracy of evil that involves a top-secret war mission in the Gulf of Mexico. (hb)

Solomon by Marilyn Bishop Shaw. Eleven-year-old Solomon Freeman and his parents, Moses and Lela, survive the Civil War, gain their freedom, and gamble their dreams, risking their very existence on a homestead in the remote environs of north central Florida. Young Solomon learns to ride a marshtackie horse and helps round up a large herd of wild cattle. (hb)

Patchwork: Seminole and Miccosukee Art and Activities by Dorothy Downs. Learn about the history of the Seminole and Miccosukee people, and how they do their crafts. Learn how to make your very own patchwork and doll, just like the Seminoles and Miccosukees—using colored paper and glue instead of fabric and a sewing machine. (pb)

Hunted Like a Wolf: The Story of the Seminole War by Milton Meltzer. Award-winning young adult book that offers a look at the events, players, and political motives leading to the Second Seminole War. It explores the Seminoles' choices and sacrifices and the treachery of the U.S. during that harsh time. (hb)

Legends of the Seminoles by Betty Mae Jumper. This collection of rich spoken tales—written down for the first time—impart valuable lessons about living in harmony with nature and about why the world is the way it is. Each story is illustrated with an original painting by Guy LaBree. (hb, pb)

A Land Remembered: Student Edition by Patrick D. Smith. This well-loved, best-selling novel tells the story of three generations of the MacIveys, a Florida family battling the hardships of the frontier, and how they rise from a dirt-poor cracker life to the wealth and standing of real estate tycoons. Now available to young readers in two volumes. (hb & pb) Teacher's manuals for both elementary and middle schools are available. (pb)

The Spy Who Came In from the Sea by Peggy Nolan. In 1943 fourteen-year-old Frank Holleran sees an enemy spy land on Jacksonville Beach. First Frank needs to get people to believe him, and then he needs to stop the spy from carrying out his dangerous plans. Winner of the Susnshine State Young Reader's Award. (hb, pb)